Always the Love of Someone

Always the
Love of Someone

Huw
Lawrence

ALCEMI ⌂

I Dan, Kath, Siôn, Eban a Molly

Thanks to Dave Browne, Ned Thomas and Catherine Merriman for their help with the manuscript.

First impression: 2010
© Huw Lawrence 2010

Published with the financial support of the Welsh Books Council

ISBN: 9780955527296

Printed on acid-free and partly-recycled paper.
Published by Alcemi and printed in Wales by
Y Lolfa Cyf., Talybont, Ceredigion SY24 5HE
e-mail ylolfa@ylolfa.com
website www.alcemi.eu
tel +44 (0) 1970 832 304
fax 832 782

CONTENTS

KEEPING ON

I had never personally known anyone who was a vagrant. It's not something you look for in life. He must have turned through my gate the minute he saw my door opening. He came up the path on worn trainers, a gaunt, balding stranger about my height with a face as long and weathered as a chimney. He was dressed normally, except for the collar of a pyjama jacket visible behind his workman's coat. I'd say he was in his sixties. He spoke with an unexpectedly melodious voice.

"I hope I find you well, sir," he said, with a gentlemanly inclination of the head. Then he confused me by staring up for too long at the 'For Sale' sign fixed to the bedroom window, so that I thought for a moment he might be a purchaser suffering some kind of sartorial amnesia. 'Highway 61 Revisited' wafted from a scratchy vinyl record of my father's. My father was a man of restricted but committed musical tastes from whom I inherited little, though everything by Bob Dylan. He'd had me for company, at least, my father. Who did I have? The surreal Dylan, singing about my life: 'Because something is happening here, but you don't know what it is, do you, Mr Jones?' God knows what my rustic-looking visitor made of Dylan's words.

"I believe I am well enough," I replied, and he returned his eyes to mine.

"Good," he said, positively. "So am I, fit as fiddle. We can give thanks." He sniffed the air, sniffed it again, then turned to me with a confidential attitude. "I do odd jobs, you know." In a firmer voice he added: "A matter of necessity." Not knowing what to say, I nodded. "Well, that's the long and the short of it," he said, looking around the garden. His eyes came to rest on the hedge. Then he looked at me, enquiringly.

"I don't know," I said. "Maybe it needs cutting."

His nose started sniffing again.

"Lentil," he murmured.

"Yes," I said, surprised, impressed even.

"Oh, I know my soups. Eat enough of 'em, make no mistake." He smiled. "Lentil is a favourite. What kind of stock did you use?"

"Ham," I said.

"That's very usual," he nodded, "Did you add one of those cubes?"

"No," I replied.

"Better still," he nodded, sniffing again.

What could I say? He was sane and sober, his odour not repellent. Apart from the pyjama collar he was just like anyone else. It wasn't as if Saturday was a busy day for me, so I said: "If you'd like some to sample, well, if you want, pull up a chair by the garden table there."

He accepted with a slight bow.

From the kitchen, through the glass door that had closed itself, I could see him with his neck craned, straining to see into the house. I thought, what the hell? I was leaving the place and anyway had nothing of great value. As I turned Dylan off, I grinned as I considered playing 'Like A Rolling Stone' for my guest's benefit, but my grin faded as I remembered my 'For Sale' sign. I filled a tray, held it in one hand while I unstuck the damned door, then carried out the whole soup-saucepan, two bowls, a loaf, a knife and a couple of spoons.

"An excellent soup maker, you are, if I may say so," he said, dipping his bread.

He didn't speak again till his soup and bread were half gone. Then he jerked his head, indicating behind him: "Hedge could do with a trim."

I pointed at the saucepan. "Help yourself."

"God bless you. I tell fortunes, too, you know."

"No thanks."

"A distressing gift," he said. "That's why I made a remark, not an offer."

"Why is it distressing?"

"Ah, so many people, these days, struggling just to keep on keeping on."

I savoured the phrase, which I had never actually heard used before, wondering if there was any advantage to having so much Bob Dylan in my head – 'Gengis Khan and his brother John / Could not keep on keeping on'.

"Your name's not John by any chance?"

"Yes," he replied, with a curious look.

"Mine's Graham," I said.

"Graham," he repeated. "A pleasure, believe me."

"Just keeping on, eh?" I sighed. "And many people, you say."

"Because you can't beat life, is why," he said, bringing his palm down on the table. "Not even when it's up and down like a cow's tail. No, sir, you can't beat it with a stick." His voice took on a canny tone. "It always seems sudden, though, doesn't it? When it comes, I mean." He gave me a look. "Whatever it is. But, still we keep on, because life is still sweet. Would you say your pergola needs a bit of fixing?"

"You can do the hedge if you want," I said.

The slight breeze pushed his hair up, silvery. "It won't cost you," he said. "It won't cost you a penny piece, no, sir. If you'll excuse me, I am hot after your good soup. Soup does make a man hot." He took off his coat and the old cardigan he wore underneath and laid them on the path and sat facing me in pyjama jacket. This riled me. Dirty clothes were one thing. Work got clothes dirty. Pyjamas, though, they were something else. Yet what could I say? What do you say to someone who sits in his pyjamas in your garden in full view of the road?

"I'm going north," he said, nodding northwards.

I said it would be colder and wetter there, thinking of when I had taken the kids camping in Snowdonia.

"You got a hedge-trimmer?" he asked.

"Just got clippers."

He gave me a look of astonishment as if I were the first person he'd ever met who didn't own a hedge-trimmer.

"It's mainly fenced. There's not that much hedge there," I remonstrated. "These gardens aren't that big."

"Valuable, though," he assured me. "If you've got kids." He craned his neck around to look into next-door's garden, then half turned to inspect the hedge behind him.

"I'm going to make a ham sandwich," I said. "Want one?"

He nodded. "Any lettuce?"

"The ham is still warm," I said.

"Forget lettuce then," he said. "Mustard would be nice."

"You want tea or beer?"

"I'd appreciate a beer," he said, with sincerity.

I fetched the ham and a carving knife, also some butter and a jar of mustard.

"Home boiled, best feed in the world," he grinned. "Rare for me, of course, home cooking." He assumed a look of bliss as he sniffed and stared at the ham. "A rare treat."

The breeze had died and the sun was directly above us. He pointed at where the table's striped parasol lay folded.

"Does that work?"

When I nodded he got up, fetched it and set it up. He tilted it, asking: "You want shade?"

I shook my head. "I like the sun."

He concentrated on eating for a while in the lavender shadow of the umbrella.

"Architect, are you?" he asked, eventually.

My eyes opened wider.

He looked cunning, leaving me to wonder for a moment. Then he chuckled and jabbed a thumb in the direction of the window. "Stuff on the table in there."

This flagrant admission that he'd been snooping irritated me.

"Did you ever used to do anything?" I asked him.

"Mechanic," he said.

"You can do that anywhere," I said, glancing at his offensive pyjamas.

"That's right," he said. "I do." He tapped the side of his head with his forefinger and then pointed it at me, as if I had seen into the mind of a genius who had become a mechanic just so as to become a tramp.

After a moment I said: "You could get a shirt for a pound or two in Oxfam."

Holding his head askew he averted his eyes skyward and then grimaced, an expression of gross embarrassment. He put his hand in his pocket and laid 38p on the table. Then he leaned back in a deliberate way, spreading his arms and legs and fingers wide apart, as if at the sky's mercy, his mouth open. He looked like a huge striped doll under my striped parasol. Then, resuming his former position, he finished his sandwich. His left forearm, facing me, revealed the tattooed outline of a girl and bore a legend. I leaned forward and read aloud: "'I love June and July.'" I looked at him.

"That's right," he said. "Don't you?"

"Not enough to have it tattooed on my arm."

He took a draught of his beer, then chuckled. "It used to be just June," he confided. "When I married, she didn't like it, her name being Rita." He plucked at his pyjama top with his fingers. "I see your point about this," he said. "Don't think I don't see your point of view. I do. Oh, I do. Let me be the first to admit it."

"I'm going to be moving house, as you may have noticed," I said. "There's a lot of clothes I'm going to be chucking out."

"I am the first to admit I need a shirt," he said, sadly. Then out of the blue he said: "Live alone these days, then, do you?"

"What gives you that idea?"

He jerked his head towards the window again. "No knick-knacks. No toys. All man's stuff."

I glared at my indiscreet window. It smiled back under an eyebrow of wisteria.

"You're observant," I said, not altogether agreeably.

"Helps with telling fortunes."

"I bet it does. What do you do, read palms?"

"Sometimes. Any method does."

"So it's all observation?" I asked.

"Well, it comes from the other person, one way or t'other, you might say."

"So there's nothing new to learn?"

"Oh, I wouldn't say that. I certainly wouldn't go so far as to say that. No, the other doesn't realise what he's saying, half the time, or even what he's doing."

I took out my cigarettes and gave him one. After a while I stood up. "I'll fetch those things," I said.

"Are the clippers in there?" He pointed to my garden shed.

I nodded. "It's open. I'll be a few minutes."

I went upstairs and put some clothes in a small suitcase that I wasn't going to have any use for. By the time I got back he was half done, clipping with quick, confident snips, as if he'd done this hedge ever since it was planted. I put the suitcase on the path, on it a disliked pair of brown shoes I had troubled to wipe over, also an old wallet, a pair of sunglasses and a straw hat he might want. Standing there, I ran my fingers through my hair, then told myself not to do that and went into the kitchen to fetch two more beers from the fridge. I sat down and watched him. It was just another Saturday, the week's shopping done. Hell, housework could wait. I'd watch football on telly later, probably in my neighbour's house, but for now I'd watch this vagrant cutting my hedge. Otherwise, well, I didn't even have the cat for company. And a tidier garden might help sell the house, of course. But I didn't want to sell the house.

He had discarded his pyjama jacket and was working stripped to the waist revealing sagged pectorals and an appendix scar. He drew on his cigarette and had a fit of coughing, after which he gasped and looked at the sky with octopus eyes. Then he worked on, observed now not just by me but my neighbour, Julian, who was pretending not to look. The vagrant took a spell, paying no attention to this other party. Slipping his pyjama jacket back on he joined me and took a draught of his new, cold beer. He gasped with pleasure then stared at the shoes. He had noticed them straight off but had carried on working. Now he gazed at them as if they were topless sunbathers.

"What size?"

"Nines."

"Thought so."

He seemed in no hurry. He accepted another cigarette, and a light, then balanced his cigarette on the edge of the table and finally tried on the shoes. I was amused by how he strove to conceal his pleasure. "A tiny bit of grass in the toes is all it's going to take," he said, soberly. He looked at me. "You know, Graham, you can forget your community projects. Just make sure everyone has a decent pair of shoes."

"I'll start tomorrow, John," I said.

He grinned and opened the case. He held a pair of trousers against himself to estimate the length. I'd put in two pairs, a few shirts, a belt, underwear and some socks. Now I remembered my gardening jacket in the shed, a garment that had never had much use. I fetched it and it fitted him very well. Not usually one for largesse, I was getting a strange kick out of this. Then the old geezer put on his trainers again, but without lacing them, and sat down to enjoy his beer and his cigarette. "The rest of the hedge won't take five minutes," he said. He nodded towards the suitcase. "This is very kind," he said, "very kind." He jerked his head towards the house. "What was her name?"

I hesitated, feeling this was intrusive. We may have got on Christian name terms somehow, but, well, after all…

"Eiddwen," I said, eventually.

"Kids?"

"Two boys."

"Gone far?"

He knew the question that mattered. What good was talk, anyway, I thought. And I didn't like the idea of my neighbour standing there. Swansea seemed far enough from Aberystwyth to me.

"Far enough," I said.

"You'll get your chance again," he said, leaning back, "whatever that's worth. Yes, you'll see some luck." He hauled smoke into his lungs and blew it out again with slow indifference. "Things go round."

"That's fortune, is it?" I asked, sardonically.

"That's about all there is to it," he nodded. "And telling it is a sight easier than living it."

"No tips about living, then?"

"Ha! Hell's fish!"

He got up and went back to the hedge, his laces trailing.

I sipped my beer and smoked. The lawn was full of dandelions. He dabbed them with weed killer from the shed. He swept up the hedge cuttings with a grass rake. He fetched the mower. Finally, he made a temporary job on the pergola with garden cord, twisting himself into some awkward shapes. When he came back to his beer I gave him another cigarette, indicating towards the chair for him to rest.

"Lord, I'm getting as stiff as an old horse," he said, sitting awkwardly.

"Were you ever married?" I asked, after a while.

"Still am for all I know." He gave a sigh. "Trouble with memories, my friend, they always make a man look bad." He gave a laugh. "As they say, 'the time so short, the craft so long to learn.' By the time a man starts to grow up, he's old, looking back at some poor little sod he feels sorry for." He stretched round in his chair to look at the garden and glance at my neighbour, who was occupied with weeding. "You'd be surprised by how little people's fortunes differ," he said. "The similarity of people's lives is truly surprising." He turned and looked at me as if certain I wouldn't have known this. Then, cocking his head to indicate behind him, he said: "His family gone too, has it?"

"Christ," I said, "How could you tell that?"

He grinned, looking at me slantwise. "I could string you along, easy," he said, "but I won't. He and his boy spent a night at a rest place for walkers in Snowdonia, somewhere I turned up. Not that he would recognise me. Hardly your friendly sort, as I recall. But I never forget a face."

"How can you know she's left him?"

"Washing on the line."

I looked at him, wondering where such talent stemmed from. Was it solitude? I thought about his life. Today, new clothes, tomorrow maybe pneumonia. What did you call that, fortune? On the other hand, he didn't feel his heart fall down a mineshaft when he woke in the morning, like I did, or my neighbour. When Julian's woman left I used to hear the poor dickhead shouting her name, 'Janet, Janet, you bitch. Where are you?' He wasn't a big guy, so you just wouldn't think he'd have room in him for such pain and rage. But he was just like the rest of us. Feelings, that's what do for us all. Bloody feelings. But this vagrant, though, his life was taken up with just himself, with just keeping on. I'd bet a pound to a wart you could bring a tear to a chicken's eye as easily as to his. He looked at it all from the outside. Was that freedom or what?

The blackbird that cheered me up when night had done its worst· landed on the hedge the vagrant had just cut, stared about with jerky movements of its head, and let out a burst of song. Did bird noises carry messages?

"So what is fortune?" I asked.

He thought a moment. "I'd say fortune is life with the blame taken out," he said.

"Who can do that?" I asked.

"It's a matter of vantage."

"You got kids?" I asked.

"Somewhere."

"My kids didn't want to be without a father," I challenged, pointlessly.

He looked at me without sympathy. "You've got some new miles ahead, Graham. Take time to swallow." He stood up, stiffly, and stretched his joints.

He took everything out of his pockets, including those of the coat on the path, till on the table next to our dishes lay a razor, a knife, a pencil stub, a toothbrush, an apple, a small can of tuna, a hunk of bread wrapped in newspaper, a can of Special Brew and an envelope sealed in cellophane with something written on it. He started unbuttoning his pyjama jacket, then pointed at the tap, asking if he could borrow some soap. I said he could use the bathroom, first on the left upstairs. He took a pair of trousers and underpants with him from the suitcase and a shirt, also his razor and toothbrush.

When he was gone I read what was on the envelope in the cellophane holder: 'In the event of my death please forward to Marjorie Mann, 14 Norton Road,' and a city I'd visited only once as a child with my father, Bristol. It made me think of Dad, his beliefs, his politics and search for purpose. It made me wonder, if each generation has to learn for itself, what kind of progress can there be? Yes, John Mann was right, it all just went round. Then he came back down and the damned door stuck again, so he rapped for me to let him out. 'And the vagabond who was rapping at my door was standing in the clothes that I once wore.' Uncanny, if you happened to have been listening to a lot of Dylan.

His trousers were perfect in length. Everything fitted perfectly. Back outside he brushed down the jacket with his hand before putting it on. I dug out an old fawn mackintosh that I hadn't worn in years. He adjusted my Panama carefully on his head, using the window as a mirror. He took a slow, deliberate look in the empty wallet. I fished out a tenner. "For the gardening," I said. It all seemed very normal, in a dream-like way. He thanked me, put my money in my wallet and transferred everything from the table to a suitcase that bore my initials. He put on my sunglasses and extended his hand. "You probably won't be here if I happen this way again, so let me wish you good luck," he said.

"I could do with as much as I can get."

"Things change, Graham," he said.

"Where are you headed today?" I asked.

He stood for a second or two as if brought up short, then just gave a crooked grin. Outside the gate he tipped his Panama to me and walked off down the sunlit street without looking back. I picked up the things on the table and carried them back into the house that I had spent twelve years paying for and was about to lose. I put 'Bringing It All Back Home' on the turntable and set it to play 'Baby Blue'. 'The highway is for gamblers, better use your sense / Take what you have gathered from coincidence…' Through the window I caught a glimpse of him walking, his suitcase in his hand, his mackintosh over his arm, his tan shoes shining, all alone, a complete unknown.

NOI

Noi arrived in Swansea in June on a six-month visa, courtesy of Roland Hughes, who signed a paper at the British Embassy in Bangkok accepting responsibility for her return. In Pattaya parlance she was long timing. She was lucky. She'd come down from Chanthaburi on the fast bus that 'falangs' like Roland called the red terror, stuffing a tiny, fashionable red rucksack with one change of clothing and some underwear. She was nineteen.

As new girls did, she sat on the pier in Pattaya South, a stone's throw from the notorious Marine Bar. She was lucky, because Roland, who was quite good looking for an older guy, decided to long time after just three nights with her. Long timing wasn't easy, neither from the girl's point of view nor the falang's. For the girl it was hard to find. For the falang it often just didn't work out, so that most men stuck to short timing, saying: "You can get the girl out of the bar, but can you get the bar out of the girl?" Noi hadn't worked out of a bar, so Roland was lucky, too. By the standards of Thai girls available for men, he'd found an innocent, a newcomer to the game.

At Gatwick and London she helped carry Roland's luggage, wide-eyed at all she saw. She had about forty English words and thirty pounds sterling. She studied coins and learned the difference between 'Ladies' and 'Gents'. It was up to her to use her wits. Unless you seized opportunity you only got somewhere in Thailand if you were already somewhere to start off with. If you weren't, it was usually a forever situation. As her mother said: "Noi, chance comes only once, maybe twice." A daughter in Europe could change the fortunes of a family.

During the hour stopover at Dubai, Noi converted the prices of the clothes displayed on the elegant mannequins into baht and asked herself what kind of a place was Thailand for a girl with ambition. Noi wanted to be something more than *noi*, which, denoting one's station, meant "little".

The front door of Roland's house was opened by an Indian child followed by its young mother, Roland's tenants. This pleased Noi. She would not, after all, be on the lowest rung of this household's ladder. She pricked up her ears when she heard that Mrs Patel's husband had been a student at the university for two years. Two years was a long time to be in the UK. Roland's friend, Sam, the thin one who lived on the top floor, explained that universities were where big amounts of learning got done.

She made friends with the Patels and tried hard to get on with Glenys, Roland's thin-lipped mother, though Glenys treated her as a servant and called her 'Little Madam'. Yet this didn't seem to matter as much as Noi at first feared. Glenys couldn't cook without spoiling the food, drank a bottle of whisky a day and was seventy-six years old. No one paid her much heed. Noi was baffled. In Thailand, Glenys would have been mistress of the house.

Sam, who explained things about Britain, was her greatest asset, except that he laughed and sang 'Here Comes the Bride' when she tugged Roland's sleeve as they passed a shop displaying wedding gowns.

★ ★ ★ ★ ★ ★ ★ ★ ★ ★

The Sea View Guest House, which did not have a sea view, was run by Roland's friend Benjamino Martinez, or more accurately by Ben's son Albert during the summer months. Noi could scarcely believe her luck in being offered a job there. Next to marriage, the two things she needed most were money and the English language. The Sea View could give them to her.

Albert's grandmother, Elen, did the ironing for the establishment. When Noi set up the second ironing board, Elen gave her English lessons. Noi called Ben 'Big Boss' and Albert 'Little Boss' and she worked very hard for Albert. If she finished early and the weather was good he would take her in his open car along the coast or to see the ponies on Fairwood Common. Roland tried to behave as though he didn't mind.

Noi worked every day, including Sunday, when the Martinez family went together to Saint David's Catholic church. She knew she was cheap labour, but she didn't mind because she didn't have a work permit. Ben, a courtly and courteous man, gave her a big bonus of fifty pounds on her birthday and a Sony Walkman.

Albert bought her small gifts, usually music cassettes. She loved music, classical, rock 'n' roll, country 'n' western, Irish folk, cajun, everything except jazz. She hated jazz. With the Walkman playing she changed the beds every day and vacuumed the Sea View Guest House from top to bottom with music in her ears. Her mind did not wander. She listened to every note. Albert told her about God and Jesus and asked her about Buddha. She told him what little she knew and asked more about Jesus, because Noi wanted to learn.

Noi was sad when Albert departed for Cardiff University in late September. She now worked for Ben. He, too, gave her presents but they were always chocolates, which Roland, who made her go out jogging every day, would not let her eat. Roland was obsessed with her weight and figure. "He want me look like boy," she complained to Albert over the phone.

Trade had fallen off at the Sea View with the passing of summer. There were times when Noi was not required. Twice she caught the train to Cardiff to visit Albert and attended dances at the University Union. She travelled back the following morning and refused to say where she'd been. Things got very bad between her and Roland. He left her to her own devices and went about his own business. In early November they would be returning to Thailand. It was already October. Noi repented. She tried nightly to soften Roland's heart with the kind of attentions she knew he liked, but it had no effect on his manner during the day. Roland no longer cared for her as before.

* * * * * * * * * *

By the time Ben telephoned Albert with worried advice about keeping Noi away from Cardiff it was already too late. By then Noi was already on a train, wearing high heels, a new mini and a tight jumper and carrying a large travelling bag. She explained to Albert that Roland had a good heart but that now she loved him, Albert. He didn't know what to do. A telephone call from Ben pointed out that Noi might not be anxious to get on the plane in November and recalled the jokes at Roland's expense when Sam had taken to humming 'Here Comes the Bride'. Ben said: "She's trouble, Albert. Send her back. You make sure you put her on the train." Albert told Noi about the telephone call and said that he was getting into trouble with his family.

In the morning Albert found a note:

"BUY BUY ALBERT. LOVE NOI. X X X."

* * * * * * * * * *

Noi spent her time at the Students' Union bar making new acquaintances. At night she hid in the toilets and then slept on chairs in one of the lounge areas. She made acquaintances who helped her place an advertisement for domestic work in the evening newspaper, and within a few days she had an interview.

Her openness made an impression on Marian Sunderland, as did the many types of work Noi could say she had done. Marian worked for a commercial group editing trade journals. She was tall but still wore high heels. She was dark-haired, thirty-something, her clothes fashionable and expensive.

The Sunderlands had a little boy, Jason, whom Noi would have to look after, along with doing the housework and some of the cooking. Noi clapped her hands. She said she was used to cooking for a family. She asked if the family liked Thai food. Marian, who liked Noi's natural exuberance, gave Noi the feeling that she wasn't going to be a servant so much as one of the family. The work she would be doing was 'help'. Help was something you *gave*. Marian in return would give Noi almost twice as much as she'd got from Ben plus her keep.

The only surprise was that the Sunderlands lived in Malmesbury. So Noi said goodbye to Cardiff. She left that same day.

On the journey down the M4 to meet Mr Sunderland, Noi asked Marian if her long black hair were dyed. She asked, she said, because Marian's eyes were blue. Thai people didn't have blue eyes, she said, unless their fathers had been American, though they all had black hair. She herself had used to have long black hair, but Roland had made her cut it short, like a boy's. She told Marian about the diet and the jogging and how Roland had made her act like a boy in bed. But she, Noi, didn't want to be a boy. She hunted through her belongings and found a photograph of herself in Chanthaburi with long hair wearing the only dress she'd owned in those days.

"You like?" she asked.

"It's lovely, Noi," said Marian, who wanted to know more about Roland, his life-style, finances and sexual preferences, everything she could learn, till she felt sure Noi wasn't likely to be getting in touch with him. A little prompting produced Noi's whole story: the decision to try her luck in Pattaya, leaving her child with her needy family; the husband who'd abandoned her, pregnant; the father who'd abused her and her subsequent transplantation to Chanthaburi at six; her rape there by Khmers at sixteen.

Marian pulled off the motorway at Exit 17. Shortly afterwards she turned into the poplar-lined driveway of her expensive home.

★ ★ ★ ★ ★ ★ ★ ★ ★ ★

Terry Sunderland was a Company Director with a small firm supplying protective enclosures to the high-growth mobile phone market. Modern communications enabled him to work from home some of the time, so Noi would be seeing more of Terry than Marian.

She liked him. He was tall, fair haired and positive. She felt sure he was very important.

Terry sipped a scotch the first evening they met, and his eyes smiled.

"How have you two been getting along?" he asked.

"She is lovely," said Noi, glancing at Marian.

"Ditto", said Marian.

"How do you like your room?"

Noi opened her eyes wide.

"It is lovely! House better than hotel."

Terry threw back his head and laughed. He had a wide, large mouth with perfectly even teeth.

Noi hoped that perhaps she was going to be lucky and he wouldn't bring up the question of her papers.

21

"We'll give it a try for a week, then, Noi, and see how we get on," he said.

"I good girl one week then get job?" asked Noi.

The Sunderlands looked at each other and smiled.

"That's about it," said Terry.

Terry decanted a bottle of St. Emilion while Marian undertook the transportation of dinner from the freezer to the microwave. Noi decided to put her heart and soul into cooking over the week to come. Terry gave her a glass of wine and showed her how to savour the bouquet.

Over dinner they asked about Thailand but she couldn't think of a thing to say. It seemed just too big a question.

So, eventually, she decided to tell them about the King and the uprising in 1992.

A thousand people had been killed in two days and then the King had commanded the two leaders to come to him. The meeting was televised. They'd had to sit on the floor before the King. Noi giggled. The military leader, getting on in years and accustomed to comfortable chairs, had difficulty sitting cross-legged on the floor, but the leader of the people, thin and humble, had been at his ease. It had made a great impression. Noi laughed happily. People had seen it on BBC television, by satellite. Her face suddenly looked scared. She'd been there, she said. She fired an imaginary automatic weapon. The military had fired into the crowd. Noi had run and then, hearing screams, had looked back at the fallen. She wasn't very old at the time, she said, just ten. She'd only gone to visit relatives. She sipped her wine, which she didn't like much, and grew calm again.

★ ★ ★ ★ ★ ★ ★ ★ ★ ★

The drive into Malmesbury for groceries took ten minutes. It was a small, pretty, very English town where foreigners stood out. Noi explored it on foot with Marian and little Jason in just half an hour after locking the shopping in the car. She'd been hoping to pay for some English tuition but Malmesbury didn't seem a likely place. Anyway, she had no transport. She'd have to learn along with Jason.

She contemplated how much more she might learn when he started school, but that was years away. She shook her head sadly and said to Marian: "Thai. School. Not learn too much."

They were in a small teashop that was otherwise empty. Marian asked: "What did you learn."

You got what you paid for it seemed, and if you couldn't pay you got very little. Noi had learned to read and write Thai and add and subtract. That and a lot of bits and pieces by rote was about all. Multiplication and division were a problem. "But can use machine," Noi said, miming the use of a calculator.

Noi had learned less at school than in her uncle's noodle soup stall in Pattaya Central, where she'd worked when she was thirteen years old, which would be twelve in Britain, she explained, because in Thailand you are one year of age when you are born. She said she had also worked on the toilets on Pattaya Soi 7, holding her hand out for five *baht* from falangs needing a pee. Every time the door of the Go-go club opposite opened she could see the girls dancing naked on the bar.

She'd been so shocked at first. "Thailand not like Pattaya town," she emphasised. "Thai people go in sea with clothes. Not show skin too much. Not wear shorts."

"Where did you go next?

"Thai Shell. Petroleum company."

"What did you do?"

"Checker. Have book. Have pen. Have hat. Write number." She outlined the shape of a hat, assumed an aloof expression, and mimed the indifferent, sideways glance of someone noting down a container number. Then she laughed with glee at the idea of herself having been such a person.

★ ★ ★ ★ ★ ★ ★ ★ ★ ★

Noi found that despite being beautiful and proud looking, Marian was relaxed and easy going. She didn't stop Noi when she was cleaning to show her how to do it, as Glenys had done. When she showed Noi how to cook Western food they did it together and had fun. They laughed a lot.

23

On Sunday morning she helped Terry in the kitchen. From him she learned to cook Sunday dinners. He was the only man with a wife whom Noi had seen cooking without it being his job. Not only that, but he did it so that his wife could lie in bed reading newspapers.

A month went by, after which Noi knew how lucky she'd been to fall in with this friendly, rich little family. The only money she spent was on birthday presents for them. She saved and sent some money home. Her English was improving rapidly. Nothing had been said about her papers. She was growing her hair long again. Soon she might splash out on some clothes. Maybe Terry would give her a lift down to London one day.

At Christmas she was like one of the family. After the turkey dinner the presents around the Christmas tree were opened. Noi had bought Jason an abacus and Marian a petticoat and a brooch. She'd got Terry a car compass and a set of snapping clockwork teeth from a joke shop, at which he laughed uproariously and picked her up from the ground by her waist and kissed her on the lips. Noi received a couple of fashionable new skirts and lingerie and a pair of gold earrings. In the evening they listened to music and danced. She danced with Marian while Terry fetched another bottle of Chardonnay and Marian ran her fingernails down her spine and squeezed her close.

On Christmas Day she got woozy and talkative. She told them how green and fertile the land was around Chanthaburi because of the rain that came from the mountains on the other side of which was Campuchea and the Khmer Rouge, and told them about the mining and polishing of precious stones, done peacefully in Thailand, but murderously over the border, where life was dangerous and there were land-mines. She described shopkeepers who spent their days peering through lenses and microscopes at tiny gems and haggling with dealers from Bangkok, and spoke of the Vietnamese district near the river, which had a church like the churches in Britain. She recounted how she'd helped her grandfather on a prawn farm and fallen flat on her face in the muddy shallows and had cried and laughed at the same time. She remembered how happy she'd been with her butterfly husband who one day never came back. "I was beautiful before baby come, small breasts, nice nipples," she sighed.

"You are now," said Marian, stroking Noi's breast. "Very beautiful. I know! Let's try on our Christmas presents."

She returned in her new petticoat. Terry and Noi were dancing close together. "Isn't it lovely," she said. "Feel the material. Why don't you try on yours, Noi?"

Noi had dreams that night in which Terry and Marian figured in that lethargic, agile way of theirs and when she awoke in their bed in the morning, her lingerie scattered about the floor, she did not know what had been real and what had been dreamt.

Early in January, before the end of the university vacation, Marian had to attend a conference at a distant town called Exeter, which lasted three days. There would be no great change, Noi would have no more responsibility than usual, because Terry would be working from home. "But," Marian said to Noi, "you'll be here in my place. Do as I do. Feel free." And she gave Noi a wink.

Noi did her chores in the same way as always. When evening came she bathed Jason and put him to bed. He was a good sleeper and rarely wanted attention after being tucked in.

As usual, Terry opened a bottle of wine. When Marian rang around eight o'clock, he said: "I love you but I'm not missing you right now, darling," and Noi heard Marian laughing down the phone.

Noi cooked a *tam yam* – ingredients like lemon grass were available in London – and then they had kluay khaek, fried banana, as a sweet dish. When they had rested and talked a bit and washed up, Terry said: "You go and put some music on, like we did at Christmas, and we'll dance, OK?"

Noi put on the music they'd danced to at Christmas. They danced so close she could feel his heart beating. Halfway through the first song he kissed her. She helped his lips to reach hers by standing on her toes.

She forgot how boring it was all day in the countryside outside Malmesbury, forgot the sameness of the identical days and parted her lips for him, remembering Marian's more gentle kiss, and, feeling safe in Malmesbury, she thanked Jesus while Terry's hands tried to reach her buttocks.

The embrace grew more passionate. She felt the pressure of his penis against her. Without a word he picked her up and carried her up to bed. He began to make love to Noi, while she parted her legs and considered how good things were, and thought of home ten thousand miles away where this happened often but where it wasn't good and always for such small rewards. Things were so different here, so much better in Britain.

KNOW YOURSELF

Small, cluttered, with hairpin-bend stairs and bedroom ceilings that follow the line of the roof, that's my cottage. Things get lost, sometimes forever, though less frequently since my wife left, unless you count her as one of them. Ivy grows outside and moss has gathered in the gutters so that they overflow. I must ask Martin Mooney to clear them. He is busy, but he'll do it. We are 'locals', I old enough to look back to when field labourers drank cold tea and many a lawyer wore a bowler. I was born in this cottage, and I became a lawyer. I rose, you might say.

Bridges and motorways bring the cities closer and everyone that comes here seems to want a dog. They want to grow vegetables, store apples, wear green wellingtons and walk a dog in someone else's fields – more dogs than you can shake a stick at. There's one that sneaks around behind you to try and nip your ankles. It makes me anxious, having been bitten as a child. "You must control your dog," I said to the owner. He apologised, but then said it was something sheepdogs did by instinct, so I pointed with my stick at the year engraved in the stone lintel above my door, 1887. "Do you think instinct was allowed to prevail back in those days?" I asked him. "Instinct puts men in jail and dogs where yours will end up if you don't teach it. Make it fear your displeasure. Train it." I turned and walked off, but the dog followed, crouching. I raised my stick, breaking into something of a sweat. I had to raise my voice to its owner as the creature started barking. "You may find our magistrates are not so soft. Have a care, sir, or you will learn how soon a fool and his dog may be parted."

My life is full of such incidents.

Recently I had to use my stick on a snapping terrier. Its owner had hysterics. You'd swear it was a child. When her husband entered my garden to threaten me with violence I was shocked. In our quiet part of Monmouthshire we are not accustomed to intimidation. "I am sixty-four, you young bully," I shrilled, almost besides myself, and I drove him off like a gander with one of the sticks my wife used for sweet peas. Then, again, when some pleasant new neighbours invited me to call, their spaniel bared its teeth and growled at me, so I said: "If you want to be welcome, you have to be nice, which includes your damned dog," and I walked away. I could go on. It would make a long list, I assure you.

People smile, as if at eccentricity. But I am a well-dressed, now retired gentleman of slight build and quiet demeanour and not in the least eccentric. Nothing untoward would ever happen to me if there were no dogs.

I have led a normal, successful life, and though it may sound like a contradiction from someone who practised criminal law, a quiet one, passed entirely in this calm village. My job revealed to me quite soon that no one is perfect. There is something the matter with everyone, the more hidden the more dangerous. That's why Plato's maxim is important: 'Know yourself'. I know very little philosophy, but I do know that much. 'Know yourself'.

Let me give you one more example, the worst one. It involved my wife, and I suspect hastened the demise of my marriage. I had agreed to represent someone who'd worked with her, a case of discrimination, and I can tell you I was charging considerably less than my usual fee. Dismissed from her post this woman had made a scene during which an exasperated superior called her 'a lunatic lesbian'. There was little to justify her reinstatement, if truth be known, but handled in the right way that epithet would have swung the case. My wife was grateful and pleasant. Maybe domestic equilibrium is achievable after all, I thought to myself, as we drove to her ex-colleague's for a consultation. But when we rang the doorbell we were greeted by a deep and angry barking.

My would-be client opened the door holding back a snarling Alsatian. "Just stand still and let her sniff you," she said. "It's because you're a man. She's a darling when you get to know her." I stood stock still while it sniffed my crotch. Then it stepped back, and, crouching as if to spring, it barked and snarled so viciously at me that its owner took it by the collar again. It strained to get at me. Slamming their door behind me I made it to my car on jelly legs. When Margaret, my wife, came through the gate a minute later the dog pushed past her barking and growling at the car. When she opened the passenger door to talk to me it pushed past her again and was trying to get into the car when I drove off, sweating and trembling, leaving my spouse to get home any way she could.

"Providence," said a colleague, "A case likes that is a can of worms, man."

"It was just a case," I shrugged. "The question is, can a wife reasonably expect a man to represent someone who attacks him with a lethal weapon?"

"Dear fellow, certainly not," my colleague chuckled, as if at a domestic tiff, as if at something I was using as an excuse, clearly not appreciating my serious point about the animal.

"They've lost their case," my wife accused, angrily. "They can't pay their costs and they're going to lose their house. I hope you're satisfied."

"Their dog lost their case," I replied. "I would have won it."

Later, she informed me that they'd had to put the dog down because no landlord would rent to them. They had been made that desperate, she accused. "It was like the child they can't have," she blamed, adding her favourite phrase, "I hope you're satisfied."

I affected surprise: "You mean they could find no home for the poor 'child'?"

Since my fear of dogs was something I never discussed, nothing was fully understood, of course, and I must have appeared remorseless. But how could I tell *her* of all people about the heart pounding and sweating nausea that the mere memory of that incident brings on? And, anyway, what is hidden is never an excuse. I recall a youth, guilty of a stabbing. He was barely five feet tall and scarcely more than a child in weight. But any connection between his behaviour and physique in the kind of community to which he had the misfortune to belong could gain him no allowances, nor did he expect any. There can never be such allowances. It is up to us to know and control ourselves.

At the same time, nonetheless, if there is law to keep us safe from each other, I cannot see why it is so rarely applied to those with dogs, when it is so readily applied to those with knives.

Margaret believes that it is not law but empathy, our humanity, that controls behaviour, that it is love not fear. She also lets me know that my own lack of it deprives me of all appreciation of what she calls the 'sublime'. Shortly before our parting I called her to account for failing to sustain this position with rational answers to rational questions, and she shouted at me: "You're not in court now, you fool. You are in my kitchen."

"Indeed?" I raised an eyebrow.

What a flood of adjectives that raised eyebrow produced, as does any reminder that we live in the house where I was born. I am told that I am 'possessive', 'insensitive', 'inaccessible', 'non-inclusive' and 'divisive'.

I have no idea why I report this in the present tense when she has, of course, gone.

Naturally, I have thought about her accusations.

In my view, empathy brings the advantages that come from being able to sense and control your own effect, but brings also the disadvantage of over-sympathising in a hostile world, making you soft. Margaret sees it only as a virtue, believing the world to be divided into those with lots of it and those with little, and she equates this with 'good' and 'bad.' Nothing in life has led me to believe things are so simple, not to mention the fact that Margaret herself seems rather short of the very quality in which she so rejoices, as witnessed by her failure to relate to our fellow villagers. Such thoughts as these eventually brought me to see that my domestic conflicts were insoluble and that a diplomatic silence was the best compromise.

Silence, alas, does not work with dogs. They do not require you to speak. Silence does not make your feelings invisible to them. The damned creatures are telepathic.

We protect ourselves as best we can.

'Know yourself'.

I enjoy a joke, sometimes, when taking a drink with my cronies in the town. I say a man should be allowed to shoot dogs on sight. I am sometimes prepared to extend it to burglars, to youths on loud motorcycles, maybe even to everyone under thirty, just to be on the safe side. They would be obliged to identify themselves with armbands till they were thirty-one. That would calm down our town centres on Saturday nights, I say. Extreme humour always gets a laugh.

'Know yourself'.

★ ★ ★ ★ ★ ★ ★ ★ ★ ★

When it became apparent that my wife after thirty-six years of marriage wasn't coming back, I eventually admitted that I liked it better that way. At first, however, the house seemed so empty that, when innocently offered one, I actually considered accepting a puppy. It would grow in my image, I reasoned, and ownership would be a way of facing my fear of other dogs. A moment's reflection despatched the idea as absurd and obnoxious, yet to have thought it at all, even for an instant, touched some chord to which I found myself reacting with vehemence. What made dogs presume to behave as if they were part of the human world? Mrs Mooney's cat had no such effrontery. Figaro spent as much time in my house as hers. When I talked to him, he purred, but he lived his own life without need of people. Why should dogs presume such demanding and dependent fellowship, and what made them go in so much for brinkmanship, almost as if they were human? Was it because they were pack animals used to social controls, which like humans they felt obliged to challenge? Looking at the unassuming, independent Figaro, I decided that solitude was a small price to pay for peace.

How am I perceived in retirement, I ask myself. As a detached sort of fellow, I suppose, thin, well dressed, rather cheerless, walking alone with a stick but no limp. I have a reputation for grumpy kindness, and, freed of an unapproachable wife with an accent as distant as herself, I find myself more closely involved with my neighbours.

Siân Mooney has no driving licence. Since her husband died she has relied on our infrequent bus service. So when her son, Martin, was in hospital I would drive her there and wait for her. She is what you'd call 'ordinary', but practical and confident. Because her hair is dyed the same auburn it always was she looks younger than I but we are almost exactly the same age. Unlike my wife, she was beautiful when young, as not many living in this village today can remember.

Never much of a one for the ladies, I was shy in that way. One admired her from afar, as they say. Not many neighbours our age can say they have known each other all their lives, since people are always moving these days. After Martin recovered, I told her that my vehicle and I remained at her disposal.

Towards the end of my career I took on fewer cases, keeping more time for myself, spending quite a bit of it on village affairs. We never had children and since my wife departed I spend willingly on emergencies. The memorial hall is more of a plague than the church roof. What they'll do when I'm dead, I can't imagine. I may fund a village trust. These days I am often brought home-cooked delicacies, and people who take foreign holidays sometimes bring me small gifts. I consider myself lucky, although, of course, such neighbourliness is a shadow of what it once was. I remember days when if I gave someone some brook trout, well, a few weeks later my mother might get a hare or a bag of apples. Those were slower and better days. These days, although the village has grown to twice its original size, there don't seem to be enough relatives anymore to take care of the old.

Siân Mooney works as a volunteer for Age Concern, assisting those no longer fully mobile and alone in their homes. To relieve her of her dependency on public transport, I made my vehicle and myself useful to her, but ended up by simply taking over one of her visits to someone in the next village. I soon found myself being asked by the organisation if I would visit someone else in that vicinity, in short, if I would join them.

How it happened, I don't know, because I had told everyone in Age Concern that I did not wish to visit any dog owners. Let them put their faith in their preferred species; let dog owning be unlucky, for once, I thought. Yet when Raymond Prosser opened his door to me, what did I find? And then what did I do? Did I turn on my heel and walk away? No, I couldn't find it in my heart. Of course, I couldn't have entered the house had the creature not been as docile as it was. After a single tail-wag of greeting it lay in its place like a piece of taxidermy quite unmoved by my nervousness.

"What is it?" I asked Prosser.

"A lurcher."

"Surely it's too big."

"A Deerhound cross," he replied, without much interest. "Not that I've ever been much of a dog man. He's only ten months, as a matter of fact. Not grown into his feet, as they say. My social worker put the idea in my head. Bad idea, of course, as things turned out. But, I must admit, he is company."

"Why a bad idea?" I asked.

"They didn't tell you?"

I shook my head.

"Well, between you and me..." He looked at me, sharply, "I mean, in confidence?"

I nodded.

"I haven't got very long. About a year, they think."

Imagining his situation, I felt shocked and dismayed. "I'm truly sorry, Mr Prosser," I said. "I don't know what to say."

"What is there to say? Nothing. It's coming to everyone. Change the subject."

"Well, then, let me say I have never heard of such a lurcher as this, but that I'm pleased he's a quiet creature and hope he remains so, since I have to tell you I have always been nervous of dogs. In fact, I asked them not to send me to where there were dogs."

"Never was a dog lover myself. I felt like you about them. But this one's very quiet, I assure you. The Deerhound is Abyssinian, I'm told, accounting for the size."

True to what he said, Ray showed little interest in talking further about his dog. He was a retired horticulturist, and before that a policeman with twenty years of service, rank of sergeant. So we shared an interest in criminal law, as well as in my garden, no longer a flower garden since my wife's departure. It is important to find common interests in this new occupation of mine. Prosser was a serious man devoid of foolish small talk and with a policeman's logical bent. He would smile at my occasional rhetorical excess. I carried out his various gardening proposals, benefiting not only from the physical exercise but also from the satisfaction of taking the garden back closer to what it was under my father's care, in those days when people relied on what they could grow, when everyone went to church and the school was open and the village and the universe were the same thing. The garden became quite an interest, both for myself and for Prosser.

He was a considerate man, always respecting my aversion to dogs. "Luther," he'd say, sharply, "move out of Alfred's way, damn you," and the dog would obey without any trace of vengeful reluctance. Prosser's attitude to it was not the usual sloppy one. One day, I brought up the matter.

"I notice you don't put much conversation in the way of the beast, Ray," I said.

"Well, it can't say anything back, can it?"

My heart warmed to him.

Eventually he expressed a wish to see my garden for himself.

Neither he nor Luther was small, but they somehow got in my car and we drove the few miles to my house, where we found Mrs Mooney doing some tidying in my kitchen. By this time she and I walked in and out of each other's houses, our back doors left open. She greeted old Prosser with pleasure and the three of us went into the garden. It was autumn and the leaves were falling.

"Tut, Alf, you need to sweep 'em up and burn them," said Mrs Mooney.

"We're all going to fall some day," said old Prosser, unexpectedly, though he seemed perky and full of interest in the garden.

Luther had wandered off into a nearby field with a copse.

"He'll be all right," assured Prosser. "He always comes to a whistle." He gave a whistle, though he didn't have much breath for it. The dog stopped, listening. "You call him," he proposed.

"Not I," I said.

Mrs Mooney pursed her lips but didn't produce enough sound to raise a mouse's ear.

With that Luther streaked off as if on a racetrack. We lost sight of him.

Prosser tried to whistle but couldn't produce any volume.

"Call him, Alf," he begged. "Please."

I put my fingers in my mouth and emitted the proud whistle I'd practised in this garden over fifty years earlier. Very shortly, Luther appeared, but stopped, reluctant to come.

"Whistle again," said Prosser.

I did, and this time Luther came in across the field at a loping canter, carrying something. He came through my gate and sat down by old Prosser, a rabbit in his mouth.

"You take it from him, Alf," said Prosser. "Give it to Alf, Luther."

Luther did, and I took it.

"Goodness. Well, I never," I said. "Good boy." I patted his head.

Mrs Mooney took the rabbit from me. "Easier done while it's still warm. You two carry on."

Prosser moved slowly and breathlessly around the garden, grunting approval of my efforts and making new suggestions. It was a mutual achievement. "Nice to feel one can still be of use," he smiled. Then, his smile fading, he pointed at the chairs on the patio near the open kitchen door, where my wife liked to drink her different brands of coffee. "There's something I wanted to bring up with you."

We sat, and there was a pause.

"You're very like I used to be," he said, eventually. "I mean with dogs. I never could be doing with them, not one bit. Then, funny thing, you know, you find they actually have a lot to offer. I wouldn't be without Luther by this time. Now, he is pretty used to you, Alf. He likes you. And, well, what I'm saying is, he is going to be around after I'm gone. You can see what I'm driving at. You're far from short, I know, but I would still insist on making sure you're never out of pocket because of upkeep. I'll make good provision."

It dawned on me that Ray was offering me his dog.

I was flabbergasted.

I couldn't actually believe he thought I'd be suitable.

"There just isn't anyone I can ask, Alf," he said, as if reading my thoughts.

I felt disturbed and uncomfortable, and it showed. My ability to disguise my feelings had deserted me. I was truly perplexed. What do you do when a friend brings up his imminent death with a request beyond conception? All right, I had conceived of owning a dog, once, for about a microsecond, but Ray couldn't know that. With no idea how to respond, I stared at the garden.

My silence dragged on.

Siân came out of the house drying her hands on a tea towel. She said briskly: "Well, it's skinned and cleaned and jointed and it's soaking in salt water for whatever you want to do with it, Alf."

"That was quick, Siân," said Ray.

She hung the tea towel over her aproned shoulder, flattened her palms against her thighs, and smiled. "I like having something to do. Takes a body out of herself. Like looking after a dog does. Alf, I'd be more than willing to help, and I'm just across the road. He'd just be another Figaro, either over here or over there."

"You're a nice lady, Siân," said Ray. "You are lucky to have her so near."

"I know," I said.

"Alf is a very nice gentleman, and very obliging, Ray, only he's always been funny with dogs since he got bit when he was little," said Siân.

"I know," said Ray.

How could they know? A voice inside told me that these people didn't know me, not the 'me' that the law courts knew and certainly not the 'me' that only I knew.

But, I reflected, that did not apply to Luther.

Dogs make their minds up straight off. They can just tell. Luther, I suspected, actually did like me.

So maybe I didn't know myself as well as I'd thought, after all.

"That rabbit would make a nice casserole," Siân suggested.

"Alf here's got more vegetables than he knows what to do with," said Ray, "sacks of spuds, clamps of carrots, strings of onions."

"I'll cook it," Siân offered.

"It'll be far too much for me," I said, "I'll need help eating it. Besides, it's not my rabbit."

"It's you Luther gave it to," Siân said, with a grin. "Alf, you're good with him, and he listens to you, and Figaro doesn't seem to mind him a bit. We'll all get on very well, like one big family."

Ray was looking hopeful again. "Believe me, Alf, he is good company. You won't have to walk him, either, if you don't want, not when he's used to it round here, what with so much woodland. You can just let him out. I'd like to be able to feel he's going to be all right, Alf."

I looked dubiously at Luther who met my eyes and cocked his head.

"You'll never be short of rabbits," Siân said. "Maybe we should wait till we've eaten that casserole, eh, Ray? That might decide him."

"You'll never have to worry about criminals, either," Ray said. "A dog this size is better than the law on your side."

GIFTS

Captain Evan Pugh-Jones was trimming his moustache in the bathroom mirror, still undressed, when the doorbell rang. He answered it barefooted, clad in a mackintosh, his white hair protruding in clumps. He was surprised to see an attractive, middle-aged woman standing wind-blown on the path.

"Mr Pugh-Jones?" she inquired. "I'm from the Estate Agents."

He had expected the sleek young man he'd talked to before, and, moreover, this was not the time arranged. The Captain was strong on schedule. He had just turned seventy-six and was strong on formality, too, and aware he wasn't yet dressed.

"I wasn't expecting you yet."

"I'm a bit early. I can come back later, if you like."

"No, no, come in."

As she entered she apologised again for being early.

"You're a woman," said the Captain, in an attempt to break the ice. "You simply don't need to apologise for being early." His laugh rose in an unexpected crescendo. As he closed the door behind her he pointed to a coconut-hair doormat on which she obediently wiped her feet.

Following him into the gloom of the front room she halted before a large, shadowy object blocking her path. Above it hung two luminescent circles of white, which she failed to interpret. When the Captain drew back the curtains, letting in some mean, February light, she found herself confronting an enormous rocking horse with an inflatable green frog taped in the saddle. The circles were the fluorescent whites of the frog's eyes.

"Sit down, please," said the Captain, clearing a space on the sofa. "Excuse me while I get dressed."

The bellowing started just as he passed through the door. She heard him grumble aloud to himself as he laboriously climbed the stairs. Looking around her she realised that the clothes strewn about among the various toys were adult-sized. The bellowing stopped. Not long afterwards the Captain reappeared, spruce in a pullover and neatly pressed slacks.

"It grieves me to sell the place," he said. He pointed to a teddy bear with buttons for eyes. "I played with that as a child in this very room." He gazed abstractedly at it. "Would you like a cup of tea before you begin?"

While he was out of the room the bellowing began again and once more the lady estate agent heard his step on the stair.

In the room there was a vintage electric train layout and toy vehicles of all sorts. Pieces of Lego were scattered everywhere. Books and board games were piled high under the window. A play-station rested on a small table. A vivid child's picture unframed on the wall caught her eye, an open-mouthed red pillar-box awaiting a floating blue letter under a yellow tree. The yellow was crayoned in zigzags, making it a laburnum, she guessed, for she knew the scene, and her recognition turned to nostalgia. In another picture next to it towering gravestones threatened a timid chapel.

Tired of waiting, she took a large tape measure out of her bag, and, moving aside some of the clutter, she made a start by measuring the room she was in.

"That's right, you carry on," said the Captain, bringing in her tea. She drank it quickly and continued surveying the house.

Every flat surface she encountered had some ornament. There were china figurines, busts, gourds, pots, carvings of animals or dark warriors and there were skins and stuffed heads on the walls and tapestries, curved daggers, swords… She recorded the house's details on to a micro-cassette, which also captured the bellowing when next it began. She was upstairs by this time and could hear the old gentleman's voice, humorous and coaxing. Then came the crashing laugh, followed by a mixture of bellows and blubbering chuckles.

The Captain appeared on the landing.

"It's all right," he said. "It's only Melville. You carry on."

He looked as though he wanted to say something else, but then turned abruptly back into the room from which he had emerged.

Entering the main bedroom, the estate agent's eyes opened wide. On a Victorian dressing table were carved and wrought boxes over-spilling with jewellery. She heard the old gentleman chuckle behind her.

"You look as though you've had a spell cast on you," he grinned.

She looked embarrassed.

"Melville never puts anything away after him."

He opened the doors of the wardrobe and gestured to her. It was crammed with costumes and dresses. He opened the lower drawer, full of brocades and silks. Enchanted, the woman thought, I hope he's insured.

"I've kept them," he said, "although my wife died twelve years ago."

"I'm sorry," she said.

He took a silk scarf with Chinese motifs, a pale green with graceful, dark dancers, and handed it to her.

"I was at sea," he said.

"I guessed."

Tossing the scarf over her shoulders, she saw it open like a graceful bird taking flight. It was a beautiful scarf.

"It suits you so well I think you should have it," he said.

She gave a small gasp.

"I couldn't," she said.

"Please."

"I couldn't possibly, no." She was adamant.

"Very well, then," he smiled, "but at least wear it for me while you're here."

From outside the room came the sound of doors being opened and banged.

"We'd better get on before he wants his breakfast," the Captain said. "I'll assist."

She worked faster with him holding one end of the tape.

"Do you have to manage without help?" she asked.

"My wife's cousin relieves me so that I get a break," he said. "She usually calls on Sundays. And Social Services provide some assistance, also some respite care."

"It must be a strain."

"I must admit it is. But it's rewarding, too." He sighed. "I'm selling to make provision while I'm still in control. The State will use up the lot, you see, when I'm gone. And then what?"

The estate agent ended up in the wildly overgrown garden, recording "mature trees" and a "restorable" greenhouse.

She re-entered the house through the kitchen door.

Inside, she found a man of about fifty with greying hair, wearing a pullover and fawn trousers. Despite the lack of a moustache, he bore a striking similarity to the other beside him. They both looked up together as she entered and she found herself looking from one to the other, for some reason aghast at the resemblance.

"I'd like you to meet Melville, my son," said the Captain. "I'm afraid I don't know your name."

"It's Julie."

Melville scrutinised the hand she extended and then shook it with deliberation. Released, she asked who had painted the pictures in the other room.

"Me."

"Is it the postbox near the cemetery gate?"

"Yes," said Melville, his face lighting up.

"When I was a little girl I lived opposite there. So, you see, I sort of recognise those pictures very well."

Melville, beaming, took her hand and shook it again.

"Was that really you making that noise before?" she asked, curiously.

Melville hung his head.

"Melville does that too often," said the Captain, "and he *must stop*."

The words had a desperate ring.

Julie, Melville's junior by some years, gave him a sympathetic grin and Melville rubbed the back of his hand against his newly shaven chin with a sly, pensive look.

Looking at her watch, Julie said with regret that she had another appointment.

As the Captain was showing her out, Melville stumbled after her proffering the two pictures she had liked.

"Oh, really, no," Julie resisted.

"You must accept them," urged the Captain, perturbed. "He'll be upset."

So she did and kissed Melville's cheek.

"It's been a privilege meeting you both," she said.

"Oh, get on with you," said the Captain. "Only promise you'll call again."

She said she would.

"No, promise," insisted the Captain. "For Melville. You needn't stay long."

So she promised.

She departed, unwittingly still wearing the scarf.

Turning back into the house the Captain's face became that of a different man. Ordering Melville to clear up the toys in the front room he trudged upstairs to make the beds. After that there was a list of chores. Just thinking of them made him tired and irritable. It was as though someone else had chatted light-heartedly with Julie.

★ ★ ★ ★ ★ ★ ★ ★ ★ ★

The institution in which they would place Melville was twenty miles away. He would get out only on minibus treats. As things were, he went out every day with the Captain, or hopefully a friend (Julie had just been earmarked as a possibility).

The cost of the institution would eat up Melville's inheritance. The Captain knew of some who had once been cared for at the State's expense but who were now homeless. He knew it because Melville had the annoying habit of making friends with them. The Captain had encountered living proofs of those newspaper reports that exposed the flaws in the government's 'Care in the Community' scheme. The Captain had entertained for some time a brooding fear that Melville might one day find himself homeless, and this had brought him to form an ambitious plan.

The plan entailed moving into a much smaller house, from which new address there would be no further contact with the Social Services. A Trust would manage the capital that would be left and friends were

43

being sought who'd visit Melville when the Captain was no longer alive.

The problematic part was training Melville.

Giant strides had been made. Melville could shop, cook, clean shoes, brush clothes, use launderettes and dry cleaners and deal with the milkman and window cleaner. He could operate a weekly budget, counting money in and out of different coloured mugs. Neighbours and shopkeepers had commented on his development. The problem was that Melville couldn't bear the constraints of daily survival, to *have* to do things when the Captain and the clock dictated. As his accomplishments grew his time for play shrank, and the more pressure the tightening daily routine exacted, the more Melville bellowed. He now even bellowed at having to get up in the morning.

The bellowing upset the Captain more than anything, because it attracted attention, which jeopardised the plan. And the more it succeeded in upsetting the Captain the more Melville did it. He didn't bellow with anyone else. The Captain succumbed to rashes, nervous ticks and an irritable bowel complaint. It never occurred to him that sharing his son's here-and-now world may have previously kept him healthy.

He told himself that apart from the bellowing everything was going according to plan.

The plan occupied a card system.

Each card had a person's name and a role, such as 'Visitor', or 'Lawyer', or 'Plumber', and referred to particular files. There was, for instance, a file labelled 'Disposals', with a category, 'Fabrics', with a list showing 'Scarves', one item in which referred you back to 'Gift 1' on a card with Julie's name on it, showing her as 'Visitor: First Stage'. If Julie fulfilled her role, further gifts would be recorded, including any that might form part of the Captain's ever-changing will.

In the event, this was not to be. For Julie never called as promised.

★ ★ ★ ★ ★ ★ ★ ★ ★ ★

On Sundays, Melville's training took them to his mother's grave.

"When I am dead," the Captain would say, "I will be buried here, too, with your mother. You must come alone, then, every Sunday."

Each time she heard this, Megan, his wife's cousin, would shake her head and purse her lips. Then the Captain would patiently explain to her for the umpteenth time how visiting the grave would give Melville adult credibility. He even took Melville to neighbours' funerals so that he'd know the procedure when the time came. Megan would look at the Captain as though he were losing his faculties, and he would wonder if she were the ideal person to be his main beneficiary. However, there simply wasn't anybody else. None of his own relatives assisted and cards with 'Visitors' on them were fewer than few. In any case, whom else did he know well enough to trust? Megan and he could look back to days very, very long ago, when, before marrying her cousin, he'd kissed her once in the garden behind the greenhouse, in another life, another world.

Megan would arrive around ten on Sunday and help Melville prepare the vegetables, while the Captain took the opportunity to enjoy some time alone and study his plan. After lunch she rested with a cup of tea in the sitting room under a train snaking through silver stars in a navy-blue sky, or sometimes she fell asleep under the smile of a golden man on a winged bicycle, pictures that had replaced those given to Julie. A quiet countrywoman, who had been granted no more than she'd expected, she wondered why she still came, with her arthritis as bad as it was.

One freezing Sunday when the Captain had a heavy cold she told him it was not his place to catch pneumonia, but that he should remember his responsibilities and keep warm. On that occasion she and Melville spent less than a minute at the graveside. As they waited outside the cemetery at the bus stop, with their breath leaving their bodies in ghostly instalments, Megan could not wait to get back to the warm house. But she was not to succeed as quickly as she hoped. Alighting from the bus in the middle of the icy, empty town, Melville started pulling her towards the far end of the terminus.

"My friends need more money in this weather," he explained, eyes wide with urgency, and he plunged his hand into his pocket to make sure he had some. "Come on."

Reluctantly, Megan followed.

There were five of them around a fire under the arches of the railway bridge.

"I don't have to shake hands when I'm with Megan," Melville informed them. Without ceremony he put all his money into the possession of a sandy haired beneficiary in an overcoat that looked like rotting cardboard. A gaunt man with a face like a ruined abbey gave Megan a look such as to convey what words could not. Another, in a cowpat cap, peered through spectacles like vandalised bus-shelters, and said: "God bless him." A fourth, wrapped in a blanket, muttered: "God bless us all," and this one gave Melville a carving of a butterfly.

Megan, shivering in her heavy coat, said: "We can't stop. We have to get back."

Thinking of the central heating awaiting her, she parted with a couple of scarce pounds of her own, only to reflect on the walk home that they could have been spent on a taxi. "Come and put my new butterfly in my treasure chest," insisted Melville, the moment they got in, pulling Megan in the direction of his room. There he opened an antique Victorian sewing-box, full of whistles, pen-knives, crucifixes, Saint Christophers, old threepenny bits, a rabbit's foot, folding scissors, shoe-horns, a pocket New Testament…

Megan picked up a battered old photograph of a family group.

"There," said Melville, pointing at a pleasant looking man in his thirties, standing with a child in each arm next to a pretty woman holding a baby. "He didn't look much like that, though. After he gave me the picture I didn't see him again." He looked hard at Megan. "The others told me he was dead. So I didn't see him."

"That's the way with death," she said. "That's just about the long and the short of it."

She gave him a hug. He was the only person she knew who received gifts from beggars.

* * * * * * * * * *

Megan returned to a damp cottage in what had become a commuter village without a shop or post office. The pain of her arthritis made her grunt as she bent to light the fire. Sitting between an electric heater and a miserable, smoking grate her feet felt as numb as two stones in a river. She clasped a mug of tea. She sat in a strange state of silent alarm associated with the mantelpiece, since the jeweller had recently supplied new quartz innards to her clock, striking her old companion dumb. It made home a different place.

"I'll go just one more time," she vowed, speaking aloud to herself, "and that'll be the last time till summer, or it'll be the death of me."

This resolve was strengthened the following Sunday.

She was caught in a downpour and had to struggle against wind and rain between the bus and the bus station café, where the proprietor was kind enough to call for a taxi.

Arriving at the house, wet and shivering, she fumbled for her purse.

"You must be Melville's auntie, then, are you?" asked the young taxi driver.

"Yes," she replied, surprised. "I visit on Sundays."

"I know," he said. "Have this one on me." He leaned across to open her door for her. "Tell Melville you got a free ride with Dennis."

She was so cold and miserable that she needed a hot bath. After that she sat in a warm Swedish dressing gown and Norwegian slippers, drinking hot chocolate in a centrally heated room whose silence was devoured by three chattering clocks of different nationalities. Above her head a golden man cycled laughing between clouds. Melville and the Captain gazed at her without speaking. She had just told them she would not be able to continue with her visits in wintertime.

Eventually, the Captain stammered hesitantly that he had for some time been trying to find the right words to invite her to come and live with them. "People won't gossip," he said. "The world has moved on from those days, and people know the situation. Besides, you're a relative."

Megan shook her head but said nothing.

"You can have any room in the house, more than one."

The Captain and Melville looked at each other, finding hope in Megan's long silence.

"That cottage of yours is damp and miles from anywhere. Come and live here and help look after us."

"And we'll look after you," added Melville.

It wasn't as if such an arrangement had never occurred to Megan. She could have got to this point any time she wanted. She just wasn't sure she could live under the same roof as Captain Evan Pugh-Jones.

"None of us is what we once were," said the Captain, as if he'd read her mind.

"Melville is," replied Megan.

She thought to herself at least one of those clocks would have to go. The whole place needed seeing to. How such an organised man could have so little ordinary gumption she just didn't know.

"You shouldn't try to change him, Evan," she said. "He's a gift to you, you know. As I keep telling you, you don't seem to realise that."

"You'd be a good influence, Megan," he replied.

Again she shook her head.

"I don't know," she said.

"Try it, a month at a time. We'll keep your place on. We'll go round there once a week to light a fire. Try it for just one month."

"Otherwise this house will be sold," put in Melville, plaintively.

"Yes, what about your grand plan, Evan?" asked Megan.

"I'll modify it."

"You can't take Melville away from this house, Evan."

There was a pause. Then he said: "If you come and live here, we'll stay." The Captain felt an unexpected release. "It would be a relief," he confessed.

Megan had no difficulty imagining how it would be. He'd have more time to spend in his study with some new plan, some new purpose, and his infernal will. Best place for him, his study. All she herself wanted was to avoid the worst and make the best of things. Living was hard enough without inventing purposes. They diverted you from enjoying what you ought to feel grateful for, like having Melville around, for instance. How could the man not see that life was something that should be made the most of? If she was alive and well, she and Melville could make a small start on the garden next Spring.

Melville gave a short, wild chuckle of anticipation.

But Megan still said nothing.

"Please say yes," blurted Melville. "Please, Megan, please."

And so, under the delighted gaze of an airborne cyclist, she did.

THE YELLOW UMBRELLA

There was no hurry to get out of bed, no one to see to but herself, and the light behind the curtains suggested there was no sun out there. Nonetheless, her letter from her sister-in-law would arrive whatever the weather, the only mail she got except for bills and junk, and there was also the chance of a chat with the postman, if he accepted a cup of tea.

She stood at the window in her brown and amber dressing gown like a bee in a jar. The boy outside by the bridge glanced up briefly at her. He was alone, his clothes ill-fitting, as with children in days gone by.

She was just finishing her porridge when she heard the postman's step. A fire in the grate had made the room warm enough to turn off the electric heater, though the day was not bright enough to turn off the light. A bunch of daffodils lit up the table. The radio chattered in different voices. Glancing through the window as she rose to her feet she saw the boy still there by the bridge, stamping and blowing into his hands like a little steam engine.

The postman dropped her letter through the letterbox and was away to his van with a wave just as the downpour began. She put the letter on the stairs, then opened the door and called to the boy. He was sheltering under the beech by the bridge behind which glowered Forestry Commission firs. He held a small yellow umbrella between the wind and his face, the smallest umbrella she had ever seen.

He hesitated.

She called again and beckoned, and this time he came, leaping over puddles that were already forming. She ushered him in, telling him to warm himself by the fire.

"Are your feet wet?"

The boy took in a stern yet anxious face with pink cheeks and prominent eyes and glanced around at the bric-à-brac and photographs, one of which showed a boy his age.

"No, they're all right, thanks."

"But you're soaked through!" she protested, with a sharp, rapid little cough. "Come on, now, take off that coat and those shoes and let's feel those socks."

He was thin and long-faced with blue eyes and sparse eyebrows that gave him a surprised look. Only the large, pink ears seemed solid and cheerful. Though he looked frail, she noticed his hands were rough. His accent and slow way of speaking told her he was as much a stranger as herself to those Welsh uplands. The pullover under his jacket was damp. She made him lay the wettest clothes out by the fire while she poured him a cup of hot tea.

"Hungry?"

Getting no reply she crossed the room to the kitchen door, put two rashers of bacon in the frying pan and set about cutting bread. "Well, what's your name and what are you doing out there all by yourself?" she called.

"Alexander, and I'm waitin' fer someone," he replied in a throaty voice. "Me dad," he decided to contribute.

The old lady's cough whiplashed. Her lips pursed. That a man should be responsible for a child and leave him to wait like that in such weather!

"Alexander what?" she queried.

"Alexander Trott."

"And what do they call you, Alex, eh?"

"Me dad calls me Alexander."

"And what does your father do, Alex?" she asked, failing to hide a note of displeasure.

"Farm work. Building work. Owt tha' turns up. There's not much to be had, so we keeps on t' move."

The boy stretched forward to peer out of the window.

"All right, all right," she reassured. "He'll not go off and leave you, I don't suppose."

She put the bacon on a plate and cracked two eggs into the pan. "How will he be coming, anyway?"

"In our van," he replied, "wi our new caravan, if he's got it."

"Well, then, you'll hear him, won't you?"

She turned the radio off. Moving aside the daffodils, she set a plateful of bacon and eggs on the table and then sat by the fire and watched him eat in silence while a fly described wide circles around the ceiling-light above his head.

He mopped up the last traces of egg and bacon fat with a piece of bread.

"Had enough?"

He nodded. "Yes, thank you very much."

She poured two cups of tea, gave the boy a wedge of fruitcake, and sat down again by the fire with an involuntary sigh. Occasionally she exploded the silence with her cough.

The boy finished eating and stretched. He stretched until it seemed his joints would crack. Then he put his socks back on.

Let him find his own way, her husband used to say to her.

With a queer revival of forgotten bitterness she remembered the agonising rapture of a smile from a dying child. She remembered forcing him to do his homework and piano practice and their arguments over bicycle excursions with friends she didn't approve of. "Oh, dear, dear me," she muttered aloud to herself, as do people who live alone, as if this other boy weren't there. The boy observed the old lady. She had adopted a gaunt, self-hypnotised stare. If she could go back, she thought, would it make things any different? Or was everything decided? Where was the justice of things. Her pistol-shot cough rang out.

"What do they call your dad, Alex?" she enquired.

"Mr Trott."

The sound of her own laughter surprised her, bringing her to herself.

"Yes, I know, I mean what's his first name?"

"Martin."

"And what did you say he does?"

"Different jobs. All sorts."

"But what sort of things, mostly?"

"I s'ppose buildin' mostly, but then there's the gardenin'. And he's good wi' cars. He's bin wi' a garage in Moelgroes last."

He pronounced the place-name correctly.

"Do you speak Welsh?"

"I learned at school."

Rising with laborious energy the old lady cleared up and washed the dishes.

"What do you do while he's at work?" she called from the kitchen.

"Depends wha' tis he's workin' at," replied the boy. Happen it'll be summat I can help wi', otherwise I goes t' school."

"School? Don't you go to school every day, then?"

He remained silent.

"Do you like it, going to all those different schools all the while?"

"Oh, I don't mind. Yes, I like it."

He didn't exactly like school, but the alternative was helping to repair stonewalls, or weeding, or rubbing down filler in damaged cars. Re-entering the room the old lady built up the fire with the remains of what was in the coalscuttle.

"I don't suppose you get much of an education, really, moving around like you do."

"I do go to school," he said.

"Every day, though? You're supposed to go every day."

A gust of rain reminded the boy to be glad he was there.

"How do you like it round 'ere?" he asked, changing the subject, for he could tell she was not local.

"It's a lovely place," she replied, "and the town's only half a mile away. There's plenty to do."

The town, the boy knew, had one street.

"How about the people?"

"I'm part of the community now," she said proudly in Welsh, her accent emphasising the wrong syllables.

"Where are you from?" he asked, continuing in Welsh.

"Worcestershire. I learned Welsh," she explained, unnecessarily. "Your Welsh is too good for me," she added. "You don't mind speaking English?"

"I am English."

"Of course," she laughed. "Where did you learn your Welsh?"

"School."

There was a silence again, followed by that sharp little cough.

"You ought to be going there every day, though," she reproved.

"Me dad teaches me, too," the boy replied. "He reckons I'm ahead on other kids me age."

"Does he now? I suppose he teaches you to read and write?"

"I can do that," the boy said, scornfully. "I'm nearly twelve."

"And your dad still teaches you?"

"He 'elps me quite a lot."

"Sums?"

"Them, aye. We're on compound interest, as a matter of fact."

"And what else?"

"Lots of things."

"What sort of things?"

"Like 'ow ter live."

"Oh, yes? And how is that?

"He teaches me that yer not happy on the want all the time, an' t'tek life as it comes. Best things in life are free. Don't mither folk. Live an' let live."

"All right, all right," replied the old lady, snappily. "You still ought to be going to school every day, though."

The boy closed his mouth and kept it closed. Slipping on his shoes, he picked up the empty coalscuttle. "It's the second one outside the back door," the old lady said. "Perhaps you'd like to chop some sticks while you're there." As he re-entered the house a few minutes later he paused with the kitchen door ajar, relocating the weight of the full scuttle across his fingers. "Don't stand there on one leg with the door open, it's draughty," said the old lady. "Bring that scuttle over here."

He returned the scuttle to its place.

"You should get a dog," he said, "or a cat."

"Wash your hands in the kitchen."

He did so, and then sat listening, hearing only the weather and the clock, while she added coals to the fire, one by one, using a pair of tongs.

"Don't you have a mother?" she asked.

"She died when I wor four," he answered. "That's when me dad took to t'road again."

"A grandmother or someone?"

"No, there's jus' me an' Dad." He glanced at the clock. "He oughter be 'ere by now."

"What time did he say?"

"He didn't say, only t' wait. But he did say happen he'd be a while."

"Why didn't you go with him?"

"The van was in Gelli being welded. No use spending two bus fares."

"What would you have done," the old lady asked, "if you couldn't have come in here?"

The boy shrugged.

"Got wet, I s'ppose."

"Do you... like it, living like you do? Being on the move all the time, I mean, all weathers. It must be hard on you."

"Oh, we do stop. Depends on what work dad's got. Sometimes we stops as long as six months or more."

"That's not what I call very settled."

A sparrow chirped. The rain had stopped and the sun came out momentarily. The boy went hopefully to the window. Against the dark olive of the firs that followed the road the bridge looked like a bright painting. Wild flowers danced in the hedgerows each side of it. The road doodled away over the moor.

"You haven't ever felt you'd like to be a bit more permanent somewhere?"

The wind shook bejewelled raindrops from the beech opposite.

"What I mean is, haven't there ever been times when you wished you might have had a proper home?"

"No."

The firs extended into the distance far beyond the other side of the bridge and somewhere beyond the firs stood a white hotel, where the boy knew his father would take a left turn before arriving at the town, where he hadn't wanted the boy to wait, lest he be questioned, the world being full of busybodies.

"A home, where things would be more regular for you, and you'd go with other kids to school every day and have friends, and proper meals, and grow up to make something of yourself. I mean, what are you going to do with yourself?"

The boy stood with his back to her and said nothing. Outside, a blackbird made being where he was sound like a bad idea. With no sign of his father, the boy sat down at the table again with a faint sigh. A dust-laden sunbeam intersected the room and the old lady told him to switch off the ceiling light. "What will you do when you're older?" her voice continued. "What will become of you in a few years? What will you do? Will you get a job? What's going to happen to you?" That voice, trembling, as if afraid of what it asked, pressed for an answer: "What's going to become of you?"

"I can't say as I miss anything nor ever thought owt on 't," the boy replied.

When his eyes next moved to the window he found that something magical had happened. A rainbow stretched across the moor framing the distant, violet mountains. The boy was entranced. The window now looked like a picture in a book. It seemed impossible that those were the mountains he and his father had just travelled through, yet he knew they were.

His father had said: "Dogs don't like travel."

A week had passed since he'd asked for a pup. That was the moment he realised he wasn't going to get one. Yellow gorse spilled down crevices. Flies were trying to get at his cheese-and-cucumber sandwich. A lizard on the rock where they sat moved, then froze and blended. His father said: "We should stop like this more often. We shouldn't try and make so many plans. We should take more time." All this had happened somewhere under the fabulous rainbow framed by the window. They were the same mountains, yet looked as if they belonged to another world. And he'd been there.

The old lady shuffled far enough forward for her mollusc eyes to register what the boy was staring at. Then she sat again.

"It's very out of the ordinary," she said.

"Aye," he said.

"I mean, a boy travelling about like you in this day and age."

And the boy thought so too and was glad.

He cocked his head, hearing the beginning of a sound he couldn't decipher.

The old lady looked at him with moist brown eyes and asked: "What's your dad like, then, Alex?"

He remained silent.

"Good with his hands, is he?" she prompted.

"Oh, aye," the boy replied, "there's nowt he canna turn his hand to." He searched for something to say. "He fitted our van out all hisself, cut holes fer t' windows, fitted glass, made the bunks an' all. You'll see it when he comes, except maybe we'll have a caravan, too, 'cause that's wha' he went fer." He faltered, trying to think of more. "Ever so good wi' engines." The noise outside he now recognised as the bleating of sheep. He's good wi' farmwork, too. Good wi' animals."

Outside, a young man's voice whooped incomprehensible instructions to a sheepdog.

"Does he have friends in these parts?" the old lady asked. "Would he stop, I mean, if he got a job here?"

Then the boy heard it, the sound of a vehicle. Slowed to walking pace behind the sheep it had approached unheard. He leapt to the window. The fly made distracted buzzing sweeps, veering around the room. The old lady's hands rose out of her lap, then fell back again.

"He's comin'," cried the boy.

He rushed to the door, then back to the old lady.

"Thank you," he said. "Thanks ever so much. But I've got to go, 'cause he'll be lookin' t' find me on t' bridge."

Then he was gone.

The old lady put on a headscarf. The boy was running towards an old white Transit that had just hauled a caravan over the bridge. Through the van's window emerged a long, apologetic face.

"I bet tha thought I wor nivver comin'."

The man spoke with jovial chagrin. The boy laughed with scornful pleasure.

A jacket sleeve raised a friendly hand. The man's face smiled. "Thank you, Missus."

The old lady turned back inside the door and saw where the boy had left his umbrella. As she picked it up her eye fell on the letter. She had forgotten all about it.

"Wait!" cried the old lady. She took a few steps in pursuit of the caravan's wide rear window, calling out and foolishly waving the umbrella, a tiny all but useless yellow umbrella left behind as if for her to wonder what to do with. The vehicle turned the corner out of sight behind the continuing firs. For a few moments the old lady stood uncertainly in the road. Then she looked up. "Won't last," she muttered, pursing her lips at the clouds in the half-rescued sky.

EXILE

It didn't look changed. The factory chimneys still rose along the soiled shore emitting nothing. For some reason his mind conjured up the Old Lodge stack being dynamited. The stack hung in the air disintegrating as it fell. He looked down at the town straggling towards its outlying villages and then looked up at the sky and sea merging beyond the coastline's industrial decay, and he thought how he still hated this place, and then hated himself for the unexpected *hiraeth* he felt at the same time.

"Home," was the word he remembered using to his area manager. The word had been out before he knew it. "South Wales," he'd corrected himself.

He'd left Manchester in a new company car and although it was a long drive he hadn't stopped, until now, when on impulse he'd pulled up in this high lay-by above the village of Furnace. He could almost make out the street he was heading for. He could picture his mother's face, slightly made up, peach coloured, with its helpless, eager eyes, its pleasure at seeing him mixed, as it would be, with uncertainty. She had a weak heart and anaemia. She was waiting for him with Joan, who had been their neighbour, and who had one kidney, chronic bronchitis and a thyroid condition. He drove down the hill into the town.

★ ★ ★ ★ ★ ★ ★ ★ ★ ★

Joan, unexpectedly fat because of her newly-diagnosed thyroid condition, offered to cook him a meal. His mother refused on his behalf and was embarrassed when he accepted without a quibble and requested coffee instead of tea. It was the custom to decline hospitality, to allow your host to insist. The conversation, variations on the theme of his mother's only son, was something he discovered he was still not immune to, though these days he was capable of more detachment

61

from it. In the two women's talk he figured like a photograph of a loved one on the wall. A short while after eating he excused himself to call on Alwyn Foster across the street, promising his mother to be back in time for them to make their family visits. Alwyn's mother, as always, was pleased to see him. She said: "We could never repay what your parents did for us."

Alwyn added: "I'd be nowhere without your parents. No one else would have helped me. We were so poor."

There had never been a father in Alwyn's life. The grand-mother had looked after the home and they had lived on a pittance earned by the mother as a clerk. His father had coached Alwyn after he'd failed the eleven-plus and this had got him into the Grammar School, and his mother had given him free piano lessons. Alwyn, now a music teacher in a Comprehensive School, recalled this, but made no direct mention of his father. Perhaps in some way Alwyn had thought of him as a father, too. Perhaps in some way he had been. His father had been pleased to see Alwyn become a teacher like himself. The two had kept in touch, and Alwyn had cried when he'd come to look at his father's body, as he himself had not been able to in an atmosphere straining to contain his mother's abandoned grief.

"Dad went very suddenly," he experimented. Alwyn nodded, but said nothing. Whatever he felt was his own affair. Still, grief made them brothers of a kind.

He offered condolences, three years out of date, on the death of Alwyn's grandmother. He stayed about half an hour, then walked back to Joan's.

★ ★ ★ ★ ★ ★ ★ ★ ★ ★

It had rained. He rang the bell three times and eventually Joan came to the door.

"Why didn't you walk in, boy?"

His mother put on her hat in front of the mirror. Joan advised her to visit both her sisters-in-law for exactly the same length of time, "So not one of them can say anything", and his mother told her that this was exactly what her mother-in-law would have said. When they opened the front door the sun was like poured steel over the wet slates of the houses opposite.

"Anytime, girl. You *know*."

"I know, Joan *fach*. I know."

His mother turned to him:

"Joan's been good to me. Marvellous she's been with me."

"Oh, no, no – "

"Yes, marvellous. *Marvellous*." As they talked the cars drove past down a blinding street, their windows like sheets of foil. "We suit each other. We like to go at the same pace. Two creaky old doors we are, Joan."

"You know what they say about creaking doors?"

"They last forever."

His mother smiled, a candle held up to a palimpsest of erased happiness. She looked at the house across the street where she had lived until eight months ago, the house in which he had been brought up.

She said, wanly: "Who'd have thought. Oh, dear. Oh, dear."

He took her arm, gently leading her to the car. "Yes, come on, Mam *fach*."

But she stopped and stared at the house.

He pointed out the cracks in the rendering, the rotten weather-boards, the grass in the gutters. He got her into the car.

He drove through a shining town.

His mother said: "I'm glad I left."

After a while she added: "This is a ghost town for me, now."

She turned to him intently, shaking her head rapidly with tiny movements. She said: "There's only Joan."

She was silent then.

* * * * * * * * * *

Auntie Maude had just returned from Spain, brown as a berry, but still ill. She'd had her breast removed. She also had heart trouble. She invited compliments on her newly-built house. From one window you could see a small corner of the estuary. The house looked unlived in. He said it was nice. She asked him how his children were. He said they were fine. Her daughter lived within two miles of him in Manchester, though they never met. Auntie Maude asked if they had seen Auntie May and his mother said the time for that visit was six o' clock.

"Why six?" whispered Maude, incredulous as a child. His mother, disturbed, said she didn't know. It was the time May had suggested. Maude looked at the clock and then at his mother. There was silence. Six o' clock, it was somehow implied, was inflexible, inhuman – to be treated so! Maude pointedly changed the subject and talked about the hotel she and Cyril had stayed at in Spain. Cyril came home and shook hands. He told Maude several times not to shout. "I'm going a bit deaf," she apologised.

Then they had boiled eggs and bread and butter.

Whether you wanted to stay or whether they wanted you to was scarcely relevant. Eventually you tore yourself away while they clung to you. Only reluctantly, and after some time, could you part, and that time wouldn't be for quite a while yet.

"I must see Dave and Kay this afternoon or I won't see them at all," he said, "so I'll slip away for an hour if you'll excuse me."

"Their little girl is his god-daughter," his mother explained.

Cyril saw him out.

He drove towards what had been the industrial side of the town. He turned left off Station Road and pulled up a little way into Robinson Street. Elizabeth would be a teenager. It was so many years since he'd called she wouldn't recognise him. There was no reply. He knocked at the house next door.

"They've gone to Australia."

He couldn't believe it.

"Do you have an address?"

"They only went two weeks ago, so there isn't one yet. They waited till the last minute because they couldn't sell the house."

He stood there.

Eventually the woman said: "Sorry, that's all I can tell you," and shut the door.

★ ★ ★ ★ ★ ★ ★ ★ ★

He drove down Y Wern past The Old Lodge housing estate where the tin-works had stood and across the intersection with Station Road into Heol Fawr, once cobbled, he remembered, with tramlines sunk in the cobbles, and on the right the works' railway lines running to the various docks. He drove past the high-rise flats that climbed out of pools of shorn grass where the Marshfield tin-works had stood, into which he had been taken as a child by his grandfather who had been a rollerman in the Wellfield. He remembered seeing the silhouettes of men lit by the heat of the furnaces. He remembered his grandfather's words when he'd learned that the works were coming down. "*Diolch i Dduw*. Thank God."

The station gates were shut. He wondered, were these the gates or were they those on the other side of the station, where the men were shot during The Railway Strike? How could he forget which gates? Their hatred of Churchill and the British Army was the only thing his two grandfathers had shared. His grandmother, hearing what had happened after the firing, had picked up her skirts and run with other women to see if her husband were dead, and now he couldn't remember to which gates she'd run. He remembered being allowed to help pull the levers in the signal box, his small hand next to the signal man's brown fist. He must have been about five. The train passed through. The gates opened.

He parked just over the railway line, in Glanmor Road, outside what had been his grandmother's home next door to the once rough and noisy Travose Head pub, which was now a private house. The chip-shop and the grocer's were gone. It had been the grocer that would once have given tick against the killing of a family pig. He could not remember a pig at the foot of his grandparents' garden though he remembered the pigsty, and there noised in his ear the memory of trucks coupling in the early morning in the lane between the garden wall and the Glanmor Foundry. His father had gone to work there at fourteen, and then, at forty, he'd gone to Trinity College, Carmarthen, and become a teacher. He remembered using the outside lavatory as a tiny child right next to the line and the trains. He remembered his grandfather killing a cockerel in the garden.

His memories were scenes of great activity. He'd wound down

the car window when he'd parked. There was hardly a sound to be heard.

Near the shore he found council houses where there had been waste ground. Beyond them he walked on levelled, grassed land with football posts and then along a path he remembered well towards a hill called the Ballast, created from the ballast dumped from ships years ago. He met an old man carrying some coils of copper wire, which at first he tried to hide. The old man had known some of his family. The wind in this place was strong enough to lean against.

"We call it Cockney Town."

His new acquaintance nodded towards the desolate new houses.

"I don't know why they want to come here."

Neville's Dock had been filled in. It was covered in scrap. Out in the mud a few black sticks showed where the pier had been. In his mind he stood on the end of the pier holding his grandfather's hand, watching the last ship ever to sail out of Neville's Dock. Her Plimsoll line was red. The sun shone on her. She had sailed for a Bristol scrap yard. He turned quickly and strode back towards his car.

★ ★ ★ ★ ★ ★ ★ ★ ★ ★

Auntie May had moved to Burry Port, but she hadn't changed, any more than Auntie Maude had, except that she, too, had grown deaf. Her house was homely. The magnificent rear view was something she left people to discover for themselves. He sat drinking cups of tea. His father's name bobbed like a lost buoy in the conversation, the original visitor, the blood relative. Then it struck him that he was that now. May mimicked his father tapping on her kitchen window in his hat and long grey mac, toothlessly mouthing a question. If she had other visitors she would nod, and he would put his teeth in before entering, or, if he'd been drinking, silently depart again. May had a memory for detail. His father seemed in some way still alive through her. His mother became more and more animated and responsive as May talked.

He had arranged to stay that night with Auntie May, and Uncle Dan offered to take his mother back to Joan's, so that he and his cousin Roy could go out for a drink.

In the Farmers Arms Roy said: "The last time I met him, he said: 'Come on, Roy, let's have a quick one.' I was supposed to be meeting Gaynor, I never did. He liked to enjoy himself."

With a start he realised that over the last ten years Roy had seen more of his father than he had.

Dan and Roy had both been put out of work. First, Fisher and Ludlow had laid men off. Then the steelworks where Roy had been a sample-passer, had closed. Eventually he had bought an old van and started a fish-round. He wasn't doing too badly. "It was a hell of a blow, terrible for a while. We thought we were going to have to sell the house, definite. A lot went to Saudi. I thought of it. But it's no life there. You plan on going for two or three years, but not many of them have come back home."

* * * * * * * * * *

She sat with her head leaning against the headrest, gazing at the upper part of the windscreen. In a weak voice she gave him wrong directions to Morriston. He knew the road well. He'd had his first teaching practice in Morriston. Teaching was something else he'd had a love-hate relationship with until he finally turned his back on it. Turning into the road leading to the crematorium, he drove towards a milky skyline. He wanted to park in the forecourt but his mother insisted that he take a leaf-strewn path that took them to the car park.

They walked slowly back through the leaves towards the building. A funeral was entering the forecourt where he would have parked. His mother said: "Somebody's in grief today." Here, a year ago, a County Councillor had gripped his hand to share his grief. "Anytime you want to come back, there'll be a job."

This was a man who in his youth, with his father and others, had fought the conditions in the old works. They had been blacklisted by their employers, had suffered, but had won in the end and become part of South Wales' Labour Establishment. His father, who had kept out of politics, always defended what had become corrupt on the grounds that it was "local control". Those arguments with his father lay behind him now. The voice of the past had stopped talking to him. Briefly in this place he heard it again, his father's voice in his head: "Look after your own square mile, my boy."

His mother had come to resurrect her grief, he to cover his with the first shovel-full of time. People could write poems about how things had been, but not for him to read. He wouldn't be there.

The cortège filled the forecourt and extended into the drive. It emptied small groups of mourners dressed in black into sudden sunshine. They looked as if they were taking part in a mime. He and his mother were in the midst of them, moving at their pace. It was hypnotic. He steered his mother round the side of the building. There two men stood smoking and one laughed. With relief he asked directions. They entered through a heavy door leading to a small room. There, under a glass panel, open at the date, they found The Book of Remembrance. His mother spread her fingers on the glass over his father's name and her face contorted silently.

His mother read some of the labels on the flowers in the room. Should she have sent flowers? Joan had said she didn't believe in it. Should she have placed a notice in the Llanelli Star? Joan didn't agree with it. What did he think? They could go down that afternoon to the Star offices... her face sagged, her eyes tugged at his.

"I don't think it matters," he said.

"Don't you, *bach*?" she replied in a distant tone.

She followed him out into the sunshine. He assisted her across the forecourt past the hearse and through the dead leaves to the car park. He opened the passenger door and supported her weight as she let herself down into the seat. The gravel crunched beneath his shoes. He slammed his door. The car moved across the car park, away from the crematorium. He was in third gear when she cried: "Oh, we didn't see Plot One."

He made a three-point-turn and drove back to the car park, where they sat, inactively. His hand reached out a little too hurriedly for the papers she finally produced from her handbag. She pulled them away and covered them fearfully with her hands. "I brought all the papers, you see," she explained, "the death certificate, everything, in case of any difficulty getting in."

She handed him a leaflet with a diagram. He looked at it.

"You've already seen Plot One," he said. "It's the lawn next to the room we were in."

He showed her on the diagram.

She began a process of elimination. "That's Plot Two. That's, th-that's... Is that Plot One?"

"No, that's Plot Six. There's Plot One." He pointed to it again.

"But I didn't know it was Plot One. It isn't the same."

They walked back through the shade and the leaves and the sunshine to the spot where they had been and they stood and looked at a neatly-shorn lawn and his mother wept. From within, came the same canned music as they had played at his father's funeral, a piano piece by Schumann played on the organ, a piece called "Dreaming".

"Gone with the wind long ago," his mother said, referring to his father's ashes.

He took her by the arm and led her back to the car. Her helplessness was her strength. It was a mode of survival. It was somehow that of Wales, too, he thought, and it accounted for the ambivalent love and inferiority Wales produced in her children. But it was too late for love now. There was nothing left to come back to. Even the language he'd grown up speaking had vanished from the streets he'd played in.

"Joan's got no-one," she said, turning to him, as they drove away from the crematorium for the second time. "She's buried her husband and hasn't got a soul in the world."

★ ★ ★ ★ ★ ★ ★ ★ ★ ★

He drove between rows of terraced houses. A woman darted into the road and drew back again quickly, a minister gesticulating from the opposite pavement. He passed over the old county border on Loughor Bridge and drove on through Bynea. In Llwynhendy old men sat on a green bench where he'd played as a boy. In Penallt he saw a familiar face, though he couldn't have put a name to it. His mother still had two visits to make, but now she decided she couldn't face them.

"We needn't have come through Llanelli at all, then," he complained. He was hungry, but he wanted to get under way. He came out of the one-way system in West End and drove over Sandy Bridge past the closed steel-works on his left and then Strade on his right. "You're going very fast," his mother said.

On his right now were the playing fields of his old school. "Isn't there a speed limit along here?" What was it he despised so much about that school? Was it really suffering seven years of dictated notes in place of teaching? Could that leave him so full of abhorrence? No, it hadn't really been the poor education, the parochial attitudes or the mediocrity. All the time it had been death. He had lived his formative years as part of a dying reality – a dying culture, a dying industry, dying politics, dying language, dying history. His father and grandfather were buried in a world as dead as fairyland. A few place-names would soon be all that was left to remind the town of its lost memory. Who wouldn't get out of such a grave? Anyway, there was no going back. Traffic to England had always been one way.

He tried to think of his wife and children waiting for him at the end of the journey, but somehow he could not escape a sense of loss and insecurity. This was a new feeling. His mother was saying what a sense of finality there had been in seeing his father's name written in the book. He forced himself to think, to analyse. His father had died a year ago. His mother had sold up and moved to be near her brother. She lived in England now. She hadn't recovered from her bereavement. They had been to look at the Book of Remembrance. He looked hard at these facts. Still something seemed wrong. What was happening?

Then he realised, and caught his breath with surprise. It was only now – for ten years he'd been deluding himself – it was only now that he was leaving home. He was seven miles from Llanelli travelling to Manchester with no reason to go back, ever. Suddenly he felt a violent, fanatical resentment.

SOMEONE DANCING

I'd go through her wardrobe in the night with a silent howl. Afterwards, around dawn, I would pick at whatever I found in the fridge

I lost weight. I missed work.

By the time my neighbour called and noticed the photographs on the kitchen table I had a series of collages made of Melanie's cut-up clothes.

Gary looked at the photographs and said: "Good God! What is she going to say? She's bound to come back for her things."

"Maybe she's already saying it."

"What do you mean?"

"Either I'm going nuts, or she came out of the front gate right before my eyes and raced off in a car. If it really was her."

"When?" asked Gary.

"Monday. I came home from work, sick. I had a temperature, though. I wasn't feeling myself. Maybe it was someone that just looked like her. Still, there was nothing posted through the letterbox or anything..."

Gary pointed at the table. "Were any of those in the making?"

"The one made out of the blue dress with the face cut from the photograph. It was on the bedroom floor."

"Hell, that doesn't look like a cheap dress. Anything gone from the house?"

"That's just it, nothing."

"Ring her up and find out."

"She won't talk to me. I always talk to the kids. I don't want to talk to them about this."

"Ask her parents."

"Jesus, I'd rather not."

It was the second time Melanie had left me. The first time her parents had offered me some vivid descriptions of myself.

71

"Didn't you call out to her?"

"I was frozen with surprise, and she was so intent on getting to her car. Before I could blink she was just a woman with short blonde hair driving off."

"What kind of car?"

"Small, silver."

"What have her parents got?"

"A silver Fiesta. But so what?"

"Yeah, right. You're sure nothing is gone? I mean, otherwise, why would she come?"

"I went through everything." I shook my head. "I started to think I was going crazy. I was sure it was her. I sniffed for perfume. I even listened to the bathroom cistern in case she'd had a pee because she's always needing one. I checked if the kettle was hot. I examined the carpets for heel marks. I checked the cheese she likes in the fridge. I stared at photographs and ornaments in case something had moved." I placed my fingers on my forehead to calm my nerves. I pointed at the photograph. "What would she think if she went into the bedroom and saw that? But I don't even know if she was here." I ran my fingers through my hair.

My skinny neighbour was giving me a look. He had pointy ears and sparse hair that curled flat on his head, same colour as his skin, and he had this strange habit of standing stock-still. You could put him in Natasha's Gallery with a plaque: 'Gary the Martian'. Jesus, I thought, *he* is giving *me* a funny look?

Anyway, what happened came about because of him.

He talked to Max Anthony, his boss at work, and next day Natasha Anthony called round. She'd opened her gallery a few years ago. She had already sold five of my pictures. I told her there was only the one I could show her, the others being fragments in a trunk. It was the last one. Sapped of energy, I'd been stepping round it for two weeks. It looked alive compared to how I felt, portraying Melanie in a leap, in her hand a tambourine of purple silk with silver bells. They were not likenesses, of course, those collages of fabric, but somehow they came close and being made of her clothes they were more real to me than representations in paint. Finally beyond the reach of crazy sorrow I could hardly remember what the experience had been like, and didn't want to.

Natasha looked at the one on the bedroom floor. She said it needed a dark velvet background. We went down to the kitchen where she studied the photographs with a mug of tea and asked if I could re-create the originals from them. I said that was the whole idea. She was tall with dyed black hair and a haughty manner and didn't look right drinking tea from a mug with a penguin on it.

She looked up from the photographs, apologised if she was being insensitive and asked what the inspiration had been, since they didn't seem to convey heartbreak or separation. I said I wasn't sure but that it seemed to me like an otherness that I forgot, that my eyes had closed to, meaning my Melanie. I said I realised this wasn't very clear but that it wasn't clear to me either. She put her head to one side and nodded encouragingly as if I were a toddler. I wasn't sure I liked her. I offered her more tea.

She asked could she come back with the velvet and some glue. She said she thought the others seemed more powerful, judging by the photographs, but preferred to start with what she could assess of the real thing. I would have to arrange the pieces on to the velvet. She produced a tape measure from her bag and we went back upstairs to take measurements.

She came next evening with a ginger-haired guy with glasses who framed the pieces that I glued to the velvet. Then he gave me a bill for thirty-five quid.

When I visited the gallery some days later Melanie sported a price tag of £400 and a 'Sold' sign.

It brings a certain feeling, selling pictures you're attached to, even of a pet or just a view. You are pleased to think of them in other people's homes and to know that they wanted them enough to pay for them. But your wife, just after she's left you?

"It's only an image," Natasha reassured, "an invention of yours."

Well, hell, yes, but what are any of us to someone else? And those images were more alive to me than Melanie herself, who wouldn't talk to me.

Natasha asked me for another. Then another.

They sold.

I reasoned with myself. You create in order to offer your creations to others, and the flipside would be a trunk full of dancing Melanies all in fragments and never to be seen.

I forgot to mention, in all of them she was dancing.

Natasha's gallery had two rooms and a basement that was usually reserved for sculptures. After selling five pictures in less than two weeks, Natasha borrowed them back, advertised, and gave the whole gallery over to an exhibition with wine and refreshments on the opening day. She opened with prices at £950 for the larger pictures. The local rag made a splash and Natasha got the exhibition into other papers and magazines. People wanted to talk to me, including the proprietor of another gallery. Critics talked of breakaway, flight, pursuit, the surprising urgency conveyed by scraps of cloth, and how extraordinary it was that she was recognisably the same person in every picture.

Every single one got sold.

I did a short TV interview. I wasn't good at this. The interviewer said the pictures didn't look planned, and I said they weren't. She said the images seemed to proclaim freedom and asked if I'd had that in mind? I said, yes. She asked what lay behind them and I said that I was still wondering that. The images were so uncontroversially loved, she said, that one couldn't help but wonder about their content. Were they about separation? I said they were just Melanie without me.

After that Natasha set about teaching me art-speak. "A bit of cred. This way you'll always have something to say even when you haven't. Harmless, Greg. Doesn't affect the pictures. Think of the sales."

Despite my short replies at the interview she said it hadn't gone as badly as it might have because I had sounded sincere. She said everything boded well for the next exhibition.

I said I didn't think there'd be one. I didn't have an idea in my head.

She laughed and said I would.

I had never thought to meet with such success or to earn so much in so short a time or become popular with people who didn't know me. I began to think about my lucky stars and the rest of my life.

Those who couldn't afford an original Melanie bought photographic prints that Natasha commissioned. She kept the exhibition open for several days after the originals had sold.

I puzzled over what made these images of Melanie so desirable.

It was an unanswerable question, but one that obsessed me, since those graceful leaps were carrying my wife away from me. What were they concealing that gave them such energy?

It was obvious when you thought about it that it was the spaces between the fragments that produced the energy holding together the leaping image. But what was it, bursting forth? What had lain behind my scissors and Stanley Knife? I could remember virtually nothing of their creation and now felt I'd even be willing to go through it again if it would answer the mystery of what touched folk enough to part them from large sums of money.

Whatever was so appealing about those nineteen images, showing Melanie's long neck angling away, her head at a determined tilt, whatever was hidden in there that made people want it, I hoped that Melanie herself had seen it. I hoped that whatever all those others saw in those images had been visible to her, too. I hoped she might even tell me what it was. I hoped it had something to do with love. I knew she had visited the exhibition, calling at a time when she knew I'd be at work. Natasha had taken her aside to tell her I was a stricken man, a hurt and therefore changed and better man. Natasha was not so bad, bless her. But it had made no difference to hard-hearted Melanie.

"Been here before, Natasha," was her reply. "You don't know him."

What did Melanie see in the gallery?

If she had been in the house that time, assuming she really was there, would it still matter what she might have thought at seeing pieces of her slashed dress on the bedroom floor? Surely a gallery alters perception. Could two halves of a dead cow take the Turner Prize in an abattoir? And my images were not lifeless, like Hirst's. Might not all those fleeing Melanies in the gallery open her eyes to the beauty of sorrowing love? Melanie could not have walked in there with an open heart like everyone else, I realised, but surely she must have seen something of what those others saw. She expressed no opinion to Natasha. She took note of the prices and talked to Natasha about the sales. When she finally did start talking to me, those were the only things she would discuss. She admitted she had been in the house that day, saying she had no sooner arrived than she spotted me through the bedroom window and left.

"Why?"

She would not discuss it.

"You must do more to support the children," she said, and this was the only discussion she was prepared to have.

"You've cashed my cheques. They were almost all that's left after paying the mortgage and the bills. How much more can I give you?"

"You're making a lot of money out of this."

"They all sold very suddenly. Natasha hasn't paid me yet. Anything, though. You can have anything. Is there any chance at all you'll come back?

"None."

"Tell me what you thought of the exhibition."

But I couldn't get her to talk about the pictures.

Nothing could get her to discuss the much-loved dance of her existence, liberated by me in cruel nights of raging, Melanie suddenly free, leaping into morning light.

"Why are you depriving the kids of a father?"

"It's over, Greg."

"They're my kids, too."

"You can see them whenever you like. But please provide more till I start work. It's not enough."

"You know what I earn and what the bills are. I'm giving you all I've got."

"I'm still looking for a suitable flat, and then I'll get work. Till then I need some of the money you've made."

"All right. You'll get it. But tell me what you think of the pictures. It might help me understand what happened to us."

She made no reply and soon the pictures became as taboo a topic as our reunion, till finally the two somehow merged.

What had she seen in those pictures?

She wouldn't say.

In the small hours, with scissors and Stanley knife to hand, I selected a garment from her wardrobe. Crouching over what Melanie had worn next to her skin, and closing my eyes, I invited again the spirit that had possessed me in those nights of creative frenzy. I didn't hope for new images, only recollection, but the slightest brush of it made me shy away. I was like a scared shaman driven back into the hut of his senses.

The experiment, however, did produce a result.

I eventually thought to take again the ruined blue dress and the photograph of the image that had come from it, the one Melanie had seen on the floor, the last one made and the first Natasha had sold. 'Controlled' and 'weak' compared to the others, the critics had said of it, and I knew why. Hampered by a re-gathering of normality, sanity and reason now resisting the extremities of lunatic grief, I had been able to complete this last image only by defying the increasing consciousness of what I was doing. This image, not so blindly made, was more within the reach of memory. Seeking to relive that struggle between unreason and reason, I held to my face the silky dress, knife and scissors ready. And suddenly there came upon me such a vicious, satanic vestige of violent glee that I snapped out of it to find myself trembling. I looked at the photograph of the fleeing dancer. The filigree bells of her tambourine seemed to tremble too.

I took from the trunk a photograph that had once stood on the dressing table, the one from which I had removed Melanie's features. As I looked from the faceless photograph to the face that was now part of that other, fleeing Melanie, I saw love's power residing not in any strength of its own but in another's freedom to reject it. Realising this, and how I had never sought to avoid it happening, I heard again my destroyed love howl its silent howl, emptiness tightening like a drum skin round my life.

BANDSTAND IN THE RAIN

Her dress is prancing wildly. The man drops a cigarette on the path of the little suburban park, treads on it and looks up. The hot weather has brewed ominous clouds, inviting things to go wrong for flimsy summer dresses. A distant rumble in the sky sends a warning the girl does not heed, though a pregnant woman with a plump child swings her stomach around to hurry past the way they've just come, a double bass with viola. You don't want to look like that, the girl squeals silently to herself, her dress misbehaving wildly. She turns as if veering away from something and gives a shiver that is not because of the wind. The man sees and grimaces.

Moments ago children played here. They are hastening away with their parents, leaving a broken kite in the grass. Everyone is heading for the road. As the man looks up at the sky his hair stages a dance on his forehead. Under his hazel eyes is a fine but broken nose. His features are set impassively. In his hand he holds a bag of the girl's things given him to carry. He is forty-four. The girl, small featured and petite, is almost twenty-three. A few yards separate them, loitering far from shelter. She stares at the rough surface of an ornamental lake behind some low railings on which she rests her hand. The others in the park hasten away, distant figures under a birdless sky. Only these two and the empty bandstand are still.

The man, gazing at the unwanted kite, finds himself staring as if he must remember it for the rest of his life, while the girl continues staring at the lake. They stand as if in a photograph, but if this were a photograph they would not be its main focus. It would be the bandstand. Abstracted in its own airy self, it merges with the darkness of the sky. It is just a shallow, conical roof with a little spire, held up on the thinnest cast-iron columns, aspiring skyward from its isolation amid shaved grass, awaiting rain.

★ ★ ★ ★ ★ ★ ★ ★ ★

The girl was drawn to her mirror three nights ago as if by some newly-remembered relative who stared at her, then winked. 'Look at the bright side,' that face told her, with a trace of a grin, 'you can't buy memories like this.' A firm little mouth under a straight nose and green irises spoke from her mirror: 'Time to decide, girl. He won't leave his wife. He's probably impossible to live with, anyway. Indecisive. Plenty of other men. Get a life.' Her mirror had proffered the same advice as her mother.

Her dress is cavorting wildly in the warm wind but there is only the man there to see. Everyone else has left the park. The girl tosses her head. One arm stiffens, fingers spiking, then they seek a new grip on the railings. He approaches her and says: "It's going to rain, you know."

She gives a high, sarcastic laugh, disturbingly buoyant.

"Are you ok?" he asks, gently.

She nods, brightly.

"How do you feel?"

"Dunno. How do I look?"

"Are you sure you're all right?"

"Yes, I'm sure I'm sure. Cut it out. People may think you're my father, but you're not."

In fact, her father is an all but unknown figure. She's seen him only a few times. The last time he gave her a glass of cider and played her a record about poisoning pigeons in a park. She was twelve. As she left she'd said: Thanks for everything.

The man says: "We'd better go."

As they follow the path out of the park the man takes the girl's hand. The rain continues to hold off. Thunder hurries them on their way.

Fate is on their side. A wide lorry has encountered a car parked some yards from the curb outside a fashion boutique and a honking queue has trapped a bus at its stop. They leap aboard just as the sky ruptures. The rain slants down like harp-strings. The bus, slowed by traffic, follows the road around the park. The lake comes into view, the colour of sheet lead. The kite is not visible. The bandstand, deserted in the rain, stands empty in its patch of mown grass, a declaration of itself alone, an image of the day.

It is just a brief summer storm. The rain becomes a light patter as the bus takes them deep into London, and even this ceases, allowing them to walk slowly to the Victoria and Albert Museum. Inside is an ominous sensation of silence. The museum's objects stare back at them. The girl's bare legs are like flickering shafts of light in the gloom. They leave to find a coffee house, then walk to the river, and on to Westminster. With time to spare they take the Underground to Kilburn. They wait in a café on the High Street.

The man casts frequent glances at the girl but what he looks for is hidden from him. She stares out of the window at the uninteresting street. Outside, they proceed with slow purpose. Red curtains billow with a life of their own from a window at the corner of an avenue. From here she insists on proceeding without him. The trees in the avenue gesticulate fervently. A wistful expression hardens on the girl's face as she turns from him and walks away, carrying her bag of things. She does not look back. He retraces his steps up Kilburn High Street.

★ ★ ★ ★ ★ ★ ★ ★ ★ ★

Having travelled to it and walked right up to it, he does not enter the National Gallery after all, but sits on the steps near a skinny old woman in a corduroy suit who is eating grapes out of a polythene bag. He sits and stares at the gleaming leather of his shoes. Pigeons fill the Square. He has drunk more coffee and smoked more cigarettes and at the Underground he tossed money into a cap for someone setting free a lively tune. Bored with his shoes he reinvests his gift of sight in passers-by, awarding marks out of ten to young females in summer dresses. He hopes Fate has put nothing unexpected on its programme, but apart from this wish avoids thinking of the girl. As he has asked her for no details, his imagination can conjure nothing fearful in relation to her unlucky reproductive organs. He thinks of the mother, met yesterday, who also has green eyes, the mother close to his own age who worries if her only daughter doesn't want breakfast. A number-plate journeying into a traffic-jam seizes his attention. Its letters spell his name. He stands. A grape heading for withered lips pauses momentarily between old fingers to stare at him like a green eye. He strides off, then runs down the steps.

Oh, for peace, for the imbecile contentment of polishing the car. In a shop he buys some small binoculars, a laser pointer and a car compass. On a poster a man with a pistol advertises a film called *The Guilty and the Dead*: 'Get rid of conscience. The rest is a piece of cake', reads the legend. In Soho he puts two pounds in a peephole and views a live masturbating woman. He walks on, wondering what he is doing there. Entering another café that has dull silver yet oddly comforting walls he drinks more coffee and smokes more cigarettes. Eventually, he asks directions to the nearest Underground.

* * * * * * * * * *

Back in Kilburn he kills an hour with a slow pint of beer and smokes. Now that he is this close, his fears are closer, also. His watch tells him to get up and start walking. He reaches the avenue. The breeze is only a distant cousin of the wind of that morning. The red curtains do not twitch. The trees ignore him. He walks till he finds the sign planted in a lawn, long grass around its feet where the mower doesn't reach: 'Marie Stopes Clinic'. The doorbell is a throaty gurgle. The door opens onto a hall with red seats and creamy cushions. He wonders whether the wearers of the white uniforms here consider their work a service or are honest servants of Pluto, god of wealth and death. The girl appears in a denim skirt and sensible shoes. "Do you come here often?" she asks, happily sarcastic. He smiles with relief. The angel of misadventure has not visited. "All done," she says, and with a gesture that is a quick flick of her hand they are out of the door walking away from the clinic's staring windows. Once again he carries her bag.

"You were very brave," he says.

She shakes her head with small, rapid movements.

"Yes," he insists.

They turn into Kilburn High Street.

"Women get a reaction, sometimes," he ventures.

"Not these days, they don't," she says cheerfully.

He glances at her. "It's not just a piece of cake, though?"

She makes no reply.

"How did they do it?"

She gives a short laugh: "So, at last he asks. Yes, piece of cake. They just put a vacuum tube up me and sucked it out."

He tries not to imagine what they sucked out.

"Were there many there?" he asks, changing the subject.

"Not quite as many as the dentist gets, I suppose."

"What were they like?"

"Ordinary. A scared teenager with her mother. The mother'd been there herself and kept saying: 'Belie-eve me, it's nuffink, darlin'.'" The girl chuckles. "And a woman with three kids already. Her feller popped in because he'd forgotten what time to call back, acting like he's Mel Gibson, and she says to me: 'Don' men try to con you, though, girl, like you're supposed to be privileged to 'ave 'em? Bless their 'ickle hearts.'" The girl laughs, adding as a non sequitur: "God the doctor was ugly."

The man is no longer sure what to say.

On the High Street they get into a taxi. He slides shut the glass panel between them and the driver. He looks at the girl's pert face, its small decisive mouth and green eyes, features that have been integral to his life for a year and a half. Although she is relieved and happy now, he still perceives distance in those features. Outside, it begins to rain.

"What was it really like?" he asks, taking her hand.

"Not as bad as I thought," she replies, candidly. "I'm glad it's over, though. The wait was awful. She gnaws her lip. Then she asks brightly: "And what did you find to do with yourself?"

He tells her about the National Gallery and the car number plate, his purchases, and Soho, even the peephole. She laughs hysterically at this. "That's what you were doing while I was having *that* done to me?" Her laughter is incredulous. She feels as if she is laughing at the world. He sits next to her, ripples of anguish showing through a foolish smile.

He presses her hand to his lips.

"Love can grow out of this like spring flowers."

The girl looks at the man who likes to make pictures with words. She wonders if he thinks 'spring flowers' can regain him access to her innermost self, where lies a fear that she may not be able to love freely again, or let herself be loved. Rain obscures the world outside the window as the girl looks at the man. When her eyes move to the streaming glass, through which little is visible, her face is empty, a declaration of itself alone, an image of the day.

ROCK BOTTOM

einir looked old beyond her years, her skin sad as laundry beneath her earnest eyes.

"It's the last of our savings, Idris," she said. "Ian and I will be able to say we've done all we can."

She did not seem stirred by much hope, more impelled by her inability to stop being Morwenna's mother.

Morwenna was going into another clinic, outside Manchester.

Meinir's manner became hesitant. "Idris, I know it's a lot to ask, but you wouldn't visit her, would you? She's said it would be better if Ian and I don't go, you see."

I took a doubtful moment or two.

She pleaded: "There's no one else I can ask"

"Well, if you think it'll do any good," I sighed, eventually.

"When do you think you can go?" she asked, pinning me down.

"Saturday," I said, reluctantly.

In the Albatross Café I complained about my lot to a group of old school friends who got together there. Morwenna, no longer the imaginative, confident beauty we were in school with, owed us all money, had lied to us all and let us all down. It was a lot for Meinir to ask, was their opinion.

I shrugged. "Yes, but imagine what's been asked of her, all these years. And, as she says, this could be the time."

"Don't kid yourself. Alwen won't like it, either."

That was the moment when I remembered that Alwen, my wife, had planned a family walk with a picnic up to Llyn Rhoshir on Saturday, and I had promised to introduce my young son to fly-fishing. No doubt the food would be spread under the lakeside's only tree, a thankfully dumb mountain ash where the beautiful Morwenna and I had made love at sixteen. I clapped a hand to my forehead. "Oh God," I groaned. "Alwen had plans for Saturday."

"Don't go."

"I can't, now I've agreed," I remonstrated. "not when Ian and Meinir can't go. How can I do that to them? I just can't."

Wrong choice, they all agreed.

There was no use delaying. I brought it up as soon as I got home.

"So that's it, then, is it?" Alwen exploded, tossing her black hair. "Just like that. Your family counts for nothing if Morwenna calls, and I suppose nothing I say can – "

"Alwen, it wasn't Morwenna. It was Meinir."

"Hell, Idris, you've made family arrangements. You've only to hear the word Morwenna and you go running."

"Alwen, we were kids. It was a lifetime ago."

Alwen threw her hand out, palm up, her dark eyes flashing. "And now that you are grown up, and it was such a long time ago, well, your family comes first, does it? Seems not."

I groaned. "Of course it does. But Meinir nursed me as a baby, Alwen, and you've known Ian and Meinir all your life, too. Who was it used to pick us up from rehearsals when we were all in the school play and drive us home? Ian did. I am doing it for them. Do you think I want to drive all that bloody way? Do you think I believe there's any point to it? You saw the woman the last time she was home. Who could possibly want her? You're being absurd, and you know it. I am going because I feel I've got no choice."

Alwen relented.

"Oh, why did it have to be this weekend?" she sighed.

★ ★ ★ ★ ★ ★ ★ ★ ★ ★

Saturday brought a warm morning with a breeze, perfect for fly-fishing. Near Cerrig Y Drudion, a remote route, I passed a thin boy of about twelve carrying a fishing rod. I thought how time goes by, recalling myself at that age, also alone much of the time, living half way up a mountain next door to Morwenna's grandmother. Memories of childhood and memories of Morwenna often arrived in the same wrapping. We had known each other all our lives. We were twelve, I remembered, kissing in the park. What could have made one life turn out to be so fortunate, the other so tragic? I told myself not to be influenced by failures in the past but to do everything I could to help Morwenna.

The walk up the steps to the mansion that housed the clinic, though, made it clear I was a fleeting visitor. Morwenna received me with her usual mixture of unease and lethargy, and as usual we talked about the old days. I held her limp, skinny hand and looked into blue eyes unalluringly tinged with yellow, recalling nothing of what I had once felt for what was now a mirage glimpsed in an outline of nose and forehead and a certain expression of her closed lips.

I squeezed her hand: "Everyone will be glad when you're well," I said. "Come home this time, where you'll get the support you need, and we'll walk from Llyn Rhoshir to Cwm Islwyn, like we used to. Just think how we'll enjoy a beer in The Raven after that long walk. You'll be full of life again, like when you were Beatrice in the school play and I was Benedick, remember? Your old self is waiting with a new life ahead, when you feel ready. You've still got your friends. Come back this time, Morwenna."

She gave my hand a faint squeeze.

"What about Alwen?"

"Alwen won't mind."

"None of it is true, Idris," she sighed. "You're the only friend I've got left in Blaen Emlyn. Probably the only real one I've got anywhere."

The words felt like a burden falling on my shoulders.

"You're wrong," I said. "Blaen Emlyn is where you belong. People don't stop belonging."

"Don't they?"

The sun penetrated the room in a faint sunbeam that lit us both, each encased in our separate skins, locked into what we were. I knew I could no more influence her than stop that sunbeam departing, yet trying had become a habit.

"Maybe people don't change, deep down," I replied. "But we can alter our behaviour. Then we become what we do. We create our own lives. We have that freedom."

She looked away, staring at the wall.

After a while she said: "I woke up in a room with dog shit on the floor. It was all over me."

There was a pause.

I didn't know what to say. Dog shit didn't seem that bad considering some situations she'd been in, but there was no way of telling what anything meant to her. She let go of my hand, muttering: "It's got to change. It's got to, now." She was hardly saying it to me. I was just there. Then there was silence.

"Have you fixed any plans for when you get out of here?" I asked, eventually.

She shook her head as if it were too much to think about.

Later I pressed my lips to her cheek: "Consider the things I said."

She nodded.

Walking towards the exit, I asked myself what the hell I thought I was doing, deceiving her about Blaen Emlyn's welcome when her drug life was over. I accused myself of saying such things for the sake of something positive to say, believing they would never be put to the test. There she was in that room, more alone than I could imagine, breathing her own atmosphere of edgy listlessness, all the goodness sucked out of her by something I wouldn't understand if I lived to be a hundred. And there was I, walking away, feeling relief, reminding myself that sucking out the goodness was exactly what she did to the lives of others, too, and that all she had ever given people since her schooldays was pain and disappointment. I thought of my disappointed family, with which I should have shared that day.

I talked briefly to the fellow who ran the clinic, a stocky guy in his forties in a black jumper and jeans, emanating a kind of benign detachment. I felt aggrieved. "She was in a place like this eighteen years ago," I heard myself say. "One weekend I found she was gone, even though she knew I was coming. I had travelled a hundred miles. Didn't see her for years, then, till next time she needed someone." He nodded, leaving my complaint hanging pointlessly in the air. "She was always so happy when we were young," I told him. "No sinister shadows or anything, I can promise you that. I've known the family all my life. She had it all, brains, beauty, talent, everything. How can someone change so much? Is it just there, another side to people, just waiting, waiting for some drug to come along."

He gave a faint smile. "Are you a relative?"

"No, a friend. A close friend."

"Addicts can come from perfect backgrounds. It makes no difference. Lots of people try drugs and no one knows why some become addicts when most don't. There are just theories. Some people believe it's genetic." He smiled again. "Our cure here does work, though. We do pretty well, here. There is hope for her, believe me. I was a patient myself and had the same treatment that she is about to begin. If there was hope for me, there's hope for her."

I suspected they were words he used often.

His voice changed. "Were you waiting for her?"

"For years, I suppose. She didn't care, though. She doesn't care about anyone."

"Addicts care about just one thing. What happened with you, yourself?"

"I married someone who does care." He touched my arm and nodded. As he turned to walk away, I asked, in a futile way: "Has she no sense of right and wrong? Can't she see the people she's hurt, and who've stuck by her for so long?"

He stopped.

"Addicts need to reach rock bottom," he said. "They must feel they have no resources left, only what they find in themselves. Support just enables them to continue. I'm glad you're her only visitor. None would have been better."

* * * * * * * * * *

On the drive home I brooded on how strange it was that I could still recall the numbness of that moment when she'd told me that her parents wanted her to concentrate on her exams and that we must stop seeing each other.

Years later, at the railway station with Ian, when we'd seen Morwenna off on the train after one of her sporadic visits, I had asked her father Ian why he'd done it.

"It just isn't true, Idris," he had replied quietly, with an unsurprised smile. "We were hoping you'd become one of the family. You nearly were in those days."

"Oh, why, then?" I had responded, wondering aloud. "It isn't as if she took up with anyone else?"

Ian had shaken his head. "What's the use, Idris?"

That's when it had first occurred to me that she might have acquired her habit as early as that sixth form play, which was when she'd ended things between us. Yet how would she have got hold of the stuff? Who from? I had tried to cast my mind back, but to no avail.

Ian had sighed. "This time, I don't mind admitting, I actually feel glad she's gone." He knew I had been seeing Alwen, and added, quietly: "Alwen is the one for you, Idris."

How long ago had that been? Twelve years ago. Poor Ian. And five years of it before that. He was still carrying the same burden, enjoying none of the normal things a man should expect from a daughter. Where was the justice of it?

As I drove home from that pointless visit, I told myself it was time to stop this. She never even showed much gratitude and it had never done any good and was never going to. She wouldn't miss me, and if she did then she had brought it on herself. What goes round, comes round. The futility of the visit made me feel even guiltier for having spoiled Alwen's family plans, and there and then I made a resolution. When the kids were in bed, I would promise Alwen that whatever she organised in the future, neither Morwenna nor anyone else would keep me from what mattered most.

A MAN AND A WOMAN

"Hi. Is that you?" she called out, smiling.

He had wound down the window of the car he had described to her on the phone. As she approached, he returned her smile. She was the one who had got out of her vehicle first. Only now did he get out of his. He felt athletic, almost as fit as the racing cyclists he'd passed on the road. He was two stone lighter than six months ago, sun tanned, with contact lenses and cropped hair. These days he was getting lots of fresh air. He sported a fashionable new shirt and jacket that he wore on dates. She wore an expensive new summer dress that made the most of her small breasts. He wasn't to know she'd bought it for the occasion.

"At your service," he said, rather awkwardly. As they walked together towards the exit to the car park he looked at his watch: "I don't know why the pubs are still shut."

"I thought we could walk by the river," she replied.

They strolled in that direction, away from the cars parked around the church at the end of the street behind them.

"It's Sunday," she said. "Maybe that's why the pubs are shut. They won't open till twelve." When they had agreed 'tomorrow' on the phone, he had not foreseen this. The whole town seemed shut. He himself never knew what day it was and lived too far out in the wilds to hear church bells. Idyllic, was the word the agent had used to describe the cottage, and it had not been an overstatement. You could fish all day and not care if you never got a take. Idyllic was the problem, if problem it was. He never went anywhere.

"I scarcely ever go anywhere," he apologised. "Who'd have guessed?"

A large, golden-haired dog trotted purposefully towards them before turning abruptly into a cobbled alley.

"Well, we're out and about now, aren't we?" replied the woman, briskly.

"Yes," agreed the man.

They were halted at the main street by a woman with a flag and they stood there watching the leaders of the cycle race speed colourfully past. Then, with a touch, the man guided the woman across the street towards a stone arch, which emerged onto a path.

"I like your dress," he said, as they set off in the only direction the path allowed.

"Thank you," she acknowledged, with poise, as if accustomed to such compliments. Being forty-seven, she wasn't.

Both turned at the hum of tyres behind them as more cyclists in shiny lycra flew across the bright mouth of the arch.

"And you enjoy life in these parts?" she asked.

"Maybe we get the life we deserve in the end. Yes, I'm happy enough, thank you, though I do tend to sink into myself a bit."

"You're too much alone, then," said the woman.

He had done none of the things he'd planned to do when he came. He'd published an article on fishing and another on country life, which at least gave him something to say when people asked what he did. What he really did was fish. Fishing concentrated your mind completely, all but taking you outside time, and then brought sudden, physical excitement. Nothing beat it. He socialised, making friends easily in his country pub. Dating agencies meant he didn't have to go without sex. What more could a man want?

"It's not good for anyone," elaborated the woman in her gentle voice.

"It wouldn't suit everyone," he murmured.

It suited him better than chaos. His wife had hated change so much she refused to replace anything. Kitchen units fell apart. Rugs covered worn patches in cherished carpets. The spare rooms were dens of inherited furniture, perches for undusted bric-à-brac, just like her mother's house had been. He'd got used to it. Such a strange mixture of tension and serenity, his wife, standing in the garden staring at the sun going down, while he himself had been always on the move, unstoppable, dragging her along after him. But she'd been patient. They'd managed to make it through twenty-eight years. Now she was alone in their big house, refusing to sell.

The woman, whose legs were bare and tanned, wore sandal-like shoes with low heels, practical for walking. Auburn hair fell to her shoulders. Care had gone into her appearance. Her tawny eyes met his with interest when she caught him taking in the curve of her breasts. However, maybe he looked a little too long at the gentle, rather equine face, because out of her mouth a pink tongue came curving, curling at the tip. So he concentrated on the steepening, downward path, aware that she was better balanced on her feet than he.

They had talked without difficulty on the phone before eventually meeting, but now she was beginning to feel unnerved by the man's lack of conversation, though he didn't seem uncomfortable. She would have preferred it if he were. She would have known what to do.

The man smiled to put her at her ease.

The path passed under a low canopy of trees, a tunnel effect she'd hated all her life, for some reason associating it with parents, church and school, and later with marriage. After her parents died and her children had grown up and left home, she herself engineered this final freedom, saying to her husband: 'We don't want to feel we're staying together just out of habit.' She explained that they'd still be married. 'You just want your cake and eat it,' he'd said. Well, she'd thought, didn't everybody? He hadn't moved anywhere nearby, though. She never saw him, now, and if she ever thought of settling down with any of the new men she saw, it didn't seem worth it. It didn't seem worth changing the known for the unknown. Anyway, she didn't need anyone, did she? She could manage alone quite happily. "Oh, hell," she heard herself mutter.

"What?" asked the man walking beside her.

"Nothing," she replied. "I wish I'd brought my straw hat, that's all, it's so sunny."

She threw him a quick glance. A pity he wasn't a little taller. He was good looking, and smart, though cumbersome a moment ago where the path had twisted steeply. She'd tried out enough men his age recently to know that bad knees were common among them.

The man didn't want to admit to himself how much his knees hurt because he had the rest of his life ahead of him and liked to dream of adventures. He had few possessions and more than enough money.

That was freedom. He could pack and leave tomorrow. Husbands eat your hearts out, here's a man who can go fishing anywhere in the world. Think of Florida, think of The Gambia, think Australia, a world of famous fishing and beautiful women lay at his feet. He was loving every minute of his new life. What was his wife doing? He knew what his wife was doing. She was gardening, and shagging his old accountant, or somebody different by now since he'd seen the accountant off with a hiding. She would never go anywhere new. Her small garden had aubrietia, alyssum, campanula, heathers, geraniums, delphiniums, pansies, lilies, you name it, she'd planted it. The borders of her tiny lawn had roses, fuchsia, azaleas, hydrangeas, a magnolia, a mallow. She crammed them all in, the devil's own gardener. He had got used to it.

"Are you happy?" the woman asked, unexpectedly.

"Yes, happy enough, thank you," he replied, and did not ask the same question in return.

The downward path grew increasingly steep. His knees slowed him. Happy? Men who'd spent their lives shouldering burdens knew when they were happy. Hours vanished beyond the clock aiming a fly, your mind pinpointed in that exact spot, the moonlit self uniting down that line with the wild fish it hunted. He couldn't tell her about such happiness. She'd probably think he should get a life. He extended a hand to help her round a nasty twist in the damned path, though she was nimbler than he. She retained his hand a fraction longer than was necessary.

"Isn't it lovely? Isn't it? Aren't these laburnum trees?"

"Yes, they're not indigenous," he replied, "or at all common. One wonders where they all came from."

A break in the trees brought a reflective gleam.

"The river," she pointed.

"That is indigenous."

She laughed readily, glad to encounter any attempt at humour.

Far above, ungainly looking cyclists struggled with the increasing, upward gradient, their bodies straining. She wondered why they did it.

The question she'd asked him niggled at the man.

He asked: "Are *you* happy?"

"I think I'm a basically happy person," she replied.

"What makes you so?"

She shrugged: "I suppose I adopt a happy outlook."

"How?"

"Maybe by not blaming circumstances. I accept things."

"Including bad things?"

She shot him a glance. "I allow fate a hand."

She wasn't sure whether she had praised a strength or explained a weakness, but she was an accepter all right, sure of very little in herself. Her husband had been an achiever, always too busy planning tomorrow to enjoy today. He got angry about everything he couldn't control, whether it was something she did, the government did, or even the weather. She didn't like to remember him behind the wheel of a car. He wasn't a bad man. Others found him amusing. Unfortunately, complaining was like pollution to her when according to him it was communication. 'Being stoical is dumb,' he'd told her. 'Life tests stoics to the limit.' And it had, in the form of him. 'A stiff upper lip is a cork in a bottle,' he said. 'People who don't express themselves get out of touch with their feelings. Then they do things and don't know why.' And maybe she had.

"Too much planning doesn't do any good," she said now, adding to her previous remark. "Something always crops up."

"I agree," the man said.

The woman looked upwards and laughed a quiet, mysterious little arpeggio, then held her tongue. The stragglers in the race above them laboured painfully. They must know they're not going to win, she thought. She felt she had begun to sense a caring, agreeable presence in this man. They were managing to be together without much trying. But then, she reminded herself, he was probably concentrating on his knees.

In fact the man's mind had turned to the sleepy town behind them, a small population that organised events in the park and the sports field and the leisure centre. The more separate lives became, the more undernourished, he now suspected. Yet, luckily, his kids had turned out well. For the sins he now recognised, he made occasional, unnecessary atonements to them. They always seemed glad to see him.

His wife, though, had been glad to see the back of him. In a last-ditch attempt at reconciliation, they had sat down together to write lists of what they liked and disliked about each other. He read the sheet of paper she handed him with dismay. 'You must hate me,' he'd exclaimed. 'I have a genuine quandary,' she'd replied. Yet she always drew back at the last moment from separating, not persuaded against it, just always wanting more time. She loved flowers. He bought her flowers. She became more and more unhappy and volatile. Listening to her snores from the next room, into which she had moved when he'd had his affair, he realised one insomniac night, while waiting for the birds to sing, that he could never console her. So in the end it was he who had done the eerie business of parting, and the relationship had ceased after all those years with the surprised gasp of a dropped accordion.

All that time in the little town behind them people had managed to share their lives more widely, not thrown back just on their own families. He'd found himself among them, like a signal box full of neglected levers. He noticed the woman by his side smile a strange, sad smile, though not at him.

The woman was thinking of all the one-sided tales she'd had to listen to about the cruelty of wives. After talking about books or music or computers, the men she met, alone and past their best years, all tried to hack the same unsuitable, obsessive route towards intimacy. So much pain. So much bitterness.

"What did you think of, just now, when you smiled?" the man asked, unexpectedly inquisitive, rather to her pleasure.

"I thought of Tchaikovsky conducting with one hand," she laughed, opening her eyes very wide as if it were the surprising truth. "He held his head on with the other. He thought it was going to fall off."

He chuckled. "Don't worry. I'd say yours is pretty well screwed on."

She hid an inward sigh. Yes, her head was screwed on, all too tight. She took no risks, and so the freedom she had sought had turned out an illusion. The battery hen she had wistfully thought of as herself had been too scared to come out when the door was finally opened. This had been the woman's discovery. What confined you, defined you – 'Teacher', 'Housewife', 'Mother', 'Neighbour', 'Arts Centre Volunteer', 'Gardener'... Oh, and that little word before her name, 'Mrs'. Could she tear down all that she was? When she had insisted on continuing her affair, her husband had said: 'You can't, and be married. Roles have rules, and if you break them the role is gone.' It was the only rule she ever did break and when he left she broke no more. She remained exactly what she was, exactly what she was regarded as being by the world she lived in.

"It's so quiet here," she said. "Do you enjoy the quiet?"

"I need away from it now and again," he replied.

"You seem very well balanced," she said, almost accusingly.

There was a demand all over the world for teachers of English as a foreign language. She'd taught it for a year in London before marrying. She had a qualification in it. She could travel. New doors would open. She already spoke some Spanish, so she could start with Spain. There was nearly all of South America. A little reconnaissance in the form of a holiday, perhaps, and then she could up stakes and go. But such thoughts always led her to admit that she felt more comfortable when she stopped thinking them. Where she liked being best was her own house, which her husband now talked about selling. She remembered how she used to forget to lock the door if she went to bed after him. He would get so angry. The woman almost burst out laughing. When she repeatedly denied having a lover, although it was obvious, her husband had gone into the wood behind the house and cried. His eyes became red and swollen. The woman had felt sad. When she told him her affair was over, he started courting her again, but then he came home unexpectedly and found her lover in his bedroom. It was the only time she'd seen him violent. She had held her head and repeated, 'Oh, the folly of it, the folly of it.' He had stared at her. 'Folly?' he'd asked. 'Is that what it is?' He gave up after that.

One more treacherous, downward turn and the path revealed a full view of the river.

"Oh, what a beautiful place!" she exclaimed.

Deciduous woodland climbed the meadows beyond the river, then gave way to a higher pasture, above which white cumulus towered along a baseline of blue. The river shone, metallically still. There came a sound like a muffled diesel, the flapping of a duck's wings, its feet trailing the water.

"You're right, the pubs do open at twelve here on Sunday," said the man. "We can have lunch any time after that."

He could not have taken this walk without the woman, could not have endured the purposelessness of not having a fishing rod in his hand. He slept when he wanted to sleep and fished when he wanted to fish. The rest of the time he read, or drove into town to buy provisions. It was wonderful. Living with someone else hadn't been so easy. His wife spent half her life searching for things she'd misplaced. She couldn't leave the house without returning for something she'd forgotten. Crockery disappeared. Cutlery got scraped with leftovers into the garbage. The shaver you thought was yours, wasn't. She apologised with the ease of a trapeze artist and then swung off on her own to somewhere distant in the big top of her brain from where she would hardly speak to you.

As the path levelled out to follow the river there came the soft crackle of last year's rotten twigs beneath their feet. The pressure was off his knees at last. He had refused to talk to his wife about his affair even though it had gone on a long time. She had moved out of the bedroom and waited. Waited for what? She'd waited for what wasn't in him, the simple ability to talk about his emotions. That was something he had learned about himself.

The woman pointed at tiny bicycles following each other at spectacular speed down the distant road cut into the hillside, sun flashing on their spokes. He thought of her, his wife, waiting, waiting for nothing, and felt a surge of sorrow. If only he'd known back then about the pause, the brief silence in which you could decide to hold your tongue, the little distance from which you learned to see, then feel less selfishly, and finally talk. The man's simple discovery had been to pause before speaking. A couple of seconds was enough to choose a better response than the one that leapt to mind, one that allowed dialogue, allowed the other's world to exist. Speech was not for you to be right. It was to find outcomes. In the absence of the right words, the pause might extend into silence, but that was better than quarrelling. The man listened these days, not so he could argue, but to understand. It was amazing what you heard once you stopped needing to answer.

The woman, watching him covertly, felt curious about this new, reflective man who said so little, this unexpectedly slim, well-dressed man whose knees she wouldn't mention.

"What makes the world go round, would you say?" she asked him.

"I suppose, communication," he replied.

She was doubtful.

"What do you think, then?" the man asked.

"Stereotypes," she replied, and sounded sad.

"Let's hope you manage to find your way round some of them."

"There's too much talk," the woman said. "It's all you get. Talk, talk, talk. The more you talk the less you face up to."

"Well, yes," the man mused. "Still, we have to respond to each other, get to trust each other by revealing ourselves."

"You're right, of course," conceded the woman, giving him a look, "or things get bottled up. Nothing gets sorted."

The man pointed to a pair of high circling kites.

"They're riding on a thermal rising from the roofs of the town," he said, "They're picking us out right now with their telescopic eyes."

"My problem is," the woman ventured, "I keep things in. I'll say I don't mind, when really I do. I accept everything. I get to feel quite remote, sometimes."

"Well, at least you don't unload yourself on to others," said the man, amiably. "Once a fault of mine, I fear. Let's sit here and rest, and enjoy the view."

The path provided benches at this point of the bank, where the river was spanned by the eyebrow curve of a slender footbridge for pedestrians. On it two bent silhouettes crossed the sky above the river's enamel gleam. Beneath them, framed within the arch, far down river, the leading cyclists approached the hump-backed road bridge.

"Can people change, do you think?" the woman asked.

"I don't know," the man replied.

"Even if we can't change ourselves, we can change our lives," she informed him. "If the wind can't be changed, our sails can."

He smiled to himself, wondering where she'd read that and how unlikely she'd managed to make it sound. She saw the smile, then followed his eyes to where an old man with an old woman on his heels were crossing the footbridge very slowly, stark-looking in dark clothes, while below them in the distance tiny bowed heads raced along the tops of distant hedgerows and shot across the river.

The old couple were crossing the bridge with such insidious slowness that the man felt his impatience rise in him. He could see nothing for them on the other side, no possible destination, so he was waiting to see which way they would turn on reaching the opposite footpath, but at this rate it would be dark by the time that pair got to the end of that damned bridge. Resisting an impulse to look at his watch, he folded the fingers of his right hand around his left thumb and closed his eyes. When he opened them again he noticed telegraph poles stalking the opposite bank. Maybe they carried a connection to wherever that old couple was creeping. It didn't matter at all how long they'd be on the bridge, he said to himself, let the sun greet them there in the morning. You couldn't hurry the present and there *was* only the present. There was nowhere to run from it, or from yourself. A fish rose. The river was so still he wondered what flies he'd choose if he were tackled up now. Yes, he would fish, fish and occasionally fuck for the rest of his time on earth. What better way of life?

From the hill behind their home, which he used to climb for the view, he had sometimes looked down at his wife in her blue bathing costume, like two drops of the sea on a petal of lawn. He felt as though he'd never really known her. People bonded for unknown reasons, buried reasons. What had the connection been? He could picture, no, he could actually feel himself hang a dry fly, dun coloured, under that fish's nose – that last rise – reading the fish, now, the water far too still to twitch the fly. This was it. Here now. Pure existence. Just being, and nothing to grasp, nothing to aim for. Yet, what *was* the connection? The woman beside him unexpectedly touched his right hand. He looked at the watch on his left. Pubs are open, he stopped himself saying.

100

The woman was staring straight ahead at the river, her face as still as the water. She had touched the man's hand not spontaneously or accidentally, but as something she had decided, so that whatever happened now, that thing would have been done by her. But nothing at all happened. Given his self-containment, then, let her reach out. Given his silence, let her speak. The river stared with its gleaming smile, part of the unseeing, unlistening world going on around her, which yet was somehow happening inside her, so that when there had come the splash of that fish it was as if it had leapt in her, and that bee had surely never hummed so loudly or birds sung at such a pitch. The man's hand, which he had not moved, lay warm against hers.

He, too, was aware of their new closeness.

Listen, about selling the house, he stopped himself saying.

Through the river's reflected sunlight and the birdsong and the bee's hum and the tremble of leaves, her words arrived.

"Come home."

PART OF THE BUSINESS

Mair sipped her coffee in the stock-room where she mixed dyes and booked appointments over the telephone. She sometimes applied the dyes, if called upon, but was glad this happened rarely. Except when asked to apply dye or sweep cut hair into a rectangular pan sunk into a corner of the floor, she was out of sight. The hairdresser's shop was in an out of the way area, which suited her. If someone she knew happened to telephone she altered the pitch of her voice and failed to find an appointment. As well as her pay, the job brought free hairdressing, which mattered to Mair. She gave no indication of how much she hated being there. She had redirected telephone calls from her home to her place of work. One such call reached her now.

The voice was that of Gwilym Llywelyn. Her heart skipped a beat. After a brief preamble he said that he might have something for her. When could they meet?

"Any evening," she said.

"This evening?"

"If you like."

"Where?"

"The White Horse."

He replied that he had it in mind to drive somewhere into the country and have a meal. That's a nice idea. We'll meet in the White Horse and decide where to go from there. That's convenient for me."

"All right, I'll wait for you outside."

"No," said Mair. "I may not be punctual. Nor might you, for that matter, and I'm not hanging around outside."

"OK. See you at seven thirty," he conceded.

After putting down the phone she felt almost as much bemused as elated, an indication of how long she'd been out of circulation. At the same time she knew better than to show gratitude.

Returning home, a little late, she was surprised to see her husband in his green uniform sprawled on the settee, watching the six o' clock News.

"What are you doing here, Gethin?" she asked irritably.

"The Alliance offices have been burgled. We can't go in till eight. What's eating you?"

"Nothing," she said. "What's on the News?"

"Motorway protests and Animal Rights."

The Alliance offices were directly opposite the White Horse, but the hell with it. Didn't she have a life of her own? She could hardly be accused of wanting to meet Gwilym Llywelyn for his own sake. It was work.

"Disgusting!" exclaimed Gethin.

"What?" called Mair, now in the bathroom.

"Just a domestic, I suppose."

"What?"

"Cardiff police just released a guy who stabbed his wife with a kitchen knife while she was nursing their baby. They gave him a caution."

"Good God!" Mair was genuinely shocked.

She walked naked from the bathroom to the bedroom.

"I don't know what the police think their job is these days," her husband called. "You get a burglary almost every day around here now."

Mair selected lingerie from a white MFI chest of drawers. Opening the doors of a matching wardrobe she began rummaging through a row of dresses.

"The cops don't go near the housing estates," her husband called.

"I know."

None of the dresses appealed to her. It seemed a long time since she'd bought a new one. "There's no money for anything," she called. She took out a dress and began to put it on.

"Recession's supposed to be over, but everybody's still struggling," he husband said.

"Not everybody," replied Mair, thinking of Gwilym Llywelyn.

"Well, we're bloody struggling. Everybody I know is bloody struggling."

Mair finished putting on the dress and examined herself in the mirror.

"Who the hell's got any future?" asked her husband.

Mair could not decide whether she liked the dress she'd chosen or not. In the other room her husband turned his head towards the open door.

"What about *our* future, Mair?"

"I know, love," she answered.

"You might try and sound as though you care." He raised his voice, resentfully. "Am I ever going to get work as a geologist? I'm a fuckin' office cleaner, aren't I? That's what I am. And that's what I'm going to be, by the looks of things."

"Oh, Gethin. I know, love."

"Is this our life, then, from now on?

"Please, don't get worked up again, Geth. I've got to meet someone."

Dissatisfied, she had taken off the dress and was trying to decide on another.

He appeared in the bedroom doorway.

"Choosing a dress is important, is it? Who for?"

"I'm hoping for some proper work," his wife replied.

Wearing the second dress she stepped further from the mirror to look at herself sideways. She congratulated herself on her figure but this one didn't do the trick, either.

"Naturally, the most important thing about getting a part is choosing a dress," he said, sarcastically.

"Not now, Gethin," she warned, with an edge to her voice.

As she tried on the next dress she said in a softer tone: "The dress is important. It's part of the business, if you're a woman."

Her husband returned to the television.

The third dress she tried was one she feared would look too young for her. That it even fitted gave her a lift. When she looked at herself in the mirror she experienced a flutter of pleasure. The fact that it was a little tight made it more revealing. She'd risk it. She slipped her gold chain around her neck, the chain with her lucky charm, and put on her highest heels. She walked into the living room. "Hey, Geth," she called, addressing the back of her husband's shock of red hair. "Turn around."

She twirled.

"Da- ra!"

He smiled half-heartedly.

She sat on the arm of the settee. He reached over and balanced on his index finger the golden sovereign suspended on the chain around her neck. He'd given it to her after working one summer cleaning university halls, whilst applying for the jobs that still had not come his way. "We are the two sides of this coin," he had said to her.

She stroked his cheek.

"It's a pity you're working, Geth, and can't meet me afterwards."

She said it although she guessed her evening would be protracted.

"I won't get home till it's light, way things are tonight. We haven't got any money in any case," he sighed. "Not that I wouldn't like to meet you, I'd love to. Anyway, enjoy yourself."

He kissed her on the cheek, lightly, so as not to disturb her make-up.

"I'll leave the car as near as I can to the Alliance. The car keys will be in the usual place," she said.

She left him sitting with his head slightly tilted as if listening for something.

She parked directly outside the Alliance offices and hid the keys in the exhaust pipe. She crossed the street and entered the White Horse with a light step. She was a few minutes early, giving herself time to check her hair and make-up and say hello to whoever might be there. The first thing she looked for was the signed photograph of herself. There it was, amongst others, staring down at her from the wall facing her at the main entrance, her old self, hair a little longer but not very different from how she looked now. Returning from the ladies' room, she glanced around. She saw a few faces she recognized, though no one she knew well enough to speak to. The pubs were all almost empty on weeknights, these days. She thought she noticed interested glances from a table of youngsters.

She sat at a window table without buying a drink, satisfied she was looking her best and comfortable with her surroundings. The interior of the old Victorian pub had been ripped out in the 'seventies and rebuilt with a circular, central bar and separate seating areas with balustrades. Mair felt nostalgically at home with the fake gaslights, tired decor and worn furnishings. She liked the scuffed woodwork. She liked the ceiling, amber from cigarette smoke. Gaming and quiz machines flashed their lights. The jukebox played 'sixties rock n' roll, the 'nineties vogue. Mair breathed the sigh of a wanderer returned to where nothing had changed.

Gwilym Llywelyn arrived five minutes late. He wore a pale suit and a striped shirt with a silk tie. He brought two drinks from the bar to show he didn't need to ask what she wanted. He put his hand on her arm and told her she looked breathtaking, told her that if anything, she had grown even more beautiful. Pleased, she took a sip of her drink. When she put it down he ambushed her hand and squeezed it.

"I've missed you," he said.

Mair gave an ironic smile.

"I mean it, Mair," he said. "When I think about you it always brings a warm feeling."

The brightness of his eyes upstaged the wrinkles beneath.

"You can't have thought of me that often or I'd have heard from you."

"You have no idea of the problems I've had to deal with since we last saw each other," he said. "I've often considered ringing you, but I'd only have been bad company. I'll tell you all about it some other time."

Mair said: "I've been gloomy, too. And sometimes I get afraid."

He stroked her hand.

"What of?"

"I don't always know. Perhaps of becoming dull. I lack challenge."

"You'll never be dull."

" I worry about my career."

"I remember how I used to," he sighed. "Those were the days."

"When have you ever had to keep the wolf from the door, Gwilym?"

He ignored the hint. "I know, only too well." He patted her hand. "Don't think I don't." He gave her hand an earnest little shake. "Always remember your talent." He might have spoken so to a newly-arrived young hopeful. However, Mair, a professional who'd been around the block a few times, felt out-manoeuvered more than affronted. "We'll have to see more of each other," he added.

Mair felt it was now clear that he still desired her. She just had to assess how much.

"That's if you can find the time, you mean, is it, Gwilym? I'm sure you have to see a lot of new talent."

His expression did not change.

"None of them holds a candle to you, Mair, and most of them aren't very attractive on the inside. You're a rarity." He nodded, seriously. "And that is not an empty compliment." He tilted his head, looking at her. Yes, she could transform a dull, stock character in the new series he was producing, if he could just get her to do it. Mair could turn a viewer's indifference into vertigo with her unexpected expressions. But this was a very small part, a big comedown from what she'd been used to. That she wanted work was obvious. He needed to assess how much.

They barely noticed the arrival of a young woman who had approached their table and now stood before them.

"You used to be Bethan Vaughan in *O Fôn i Fynwy*," she said, naming a popular soap opera. "I knew you straight away, though my friends wouldn't believe me." She extended paper and a ball-point pen. "Could I have your autograph, d'you think?"

Gwilym Llywelyn was in a public place holding the hand of a beautiful actress who was not his wife. He leaned back in his chair. As Mair signed her name, others of the girl's group intruded with the same request. Uninvolved, the camera in Gwilym Llywelyn's mind exaggerated Mair's imperfections, the slightly-flared nostrils, the heavy chin and graceless arms that summed up why he'd thought of her. As well as being mysterious and haughty-looking, she was also ordinary, an unusual combination that might rescue the small and colourless part he had in mind.

When she'd finished signing autographs he indicated towards the door and rose to his feet.

"Let's go."

His tone was authoritative.

In a little known restaurant some six or seven miles outside the city, a passable wine and a good meal produced a feeling of relaxed wellbeing in Gwilym Llywelyn. He had made a passing reference to a possible part. She had merely raised an eyebrow. She'd made no reference to his telephone call. He knew that an affronted "no" from her would be a problem, but if she proved even slightly hesitant he could promise her something extra. He didn't want to do that unless it was necessary. She was slightly intoxicated as they walked across the car park, his arm around her waist, but had still given him nothing to go on. He drove back to the city with one hand on the steering wheel and the other on her knee. "I wish we were in France," he said. "On a boat, on a canal or a river, going from café to café, restaurant to restaurant."

"What a wonderful dream," sighed Mair, more interested in how at the end of the main course he'd let slip there was a new series. But he had not then returned to the subject.

"Shall we make it come true, sometime?" he said.

"It would be lovely, wouldn't it?" she said. "Despite myself, I find I've forgiven you for ignoring me so long."

"Well," he smiled, "after all, I've forgiven you for dropping me."

She put her hand on his thigh and said: "Things got complicated, Gwilym. I thought you'd understood. I'm married, too, remember."

She wouldn't drop him this time, she decided. What were a few hours in a hotel now and again if it kept you in work?

Gwilym Llywelyn liked what she'd said. It meant no dangerous ties.

He squeezed her knee again, wishing he knew more about her

circumstances. "It's difficult when you care for more than one person, when you have responsibilities," he said.

"Exactly," she sighed.

"What's your husband doing these days, Mair?"

"He's changing jobs, moving to some mining company. But let's not talk about our other lives, Gwilym. Really, let's not. It's upsetting."

"Quite right," he murmured. He stroked her knee. "I'm so glad we've got together again. And don't worry about the future," he added.

Mair knew that he had not taken her out that evening with anything more than dinner in mind, and the need to fill a part that probably wasn't much good, or he'd have made capital of it, but there was the future, and now that the right chords had been struck why not get the business over and done with, signed and sealed as it were, fate having provided an empty flat.

"At the moment I'm a mite too tiddly to be worrying about the future, Gwilym," she replied with a giggle. "I'm more worried about getting up the stairs to the flat in these heels. You'll have to hold on to me if you're coming in for coffee." The car was already in the neighbourhood where she lived. "Gethin's away with this new job," she added.

"When's he due back?"

"Not till tomorrow."

He had a stock of excuses that covered him till about one a.m. and the dashboard clock told him that it was nineteen minutes past ten.

A short time later he was sitting on a settee with loose covers, his mind on the soft, fleshy curves inside Mair's dress as he watched her carry coffee in from the kitchen. A framed mountain scene in oils hung above the mantelpiece. The other walls were hung with woodland scenes in chipped frames, water-colours from the early decades of the century. In a corner of the room the mellow varnish and sumptuous shape of a cello was embraced by a trailing houseplant. Mair set down two old and beautiful cups and saucers and a matching milk-jug.

"You don't take sugar, do you?"

"No."

She sat next to him on the settee and gave a tipsy smile. "Sweet enough already, are you?"

He leaned towards her and kissed her wide, curved mouth, noting the peppermint which told him she had just cleaned her teeth, for she smoked. She put her arms around him and drew him closer and ran her fingers through his dyed hair. After a while they drew apart and sipped their coffee.

"Who plays the cello?"

"I do."

She thought of the times she'd almost sold it. Now was getting to be one of those times.

"There's so much I don't know about you," he said.

He put his arm around her shoulder again.

"I don't want you to think I'm holding out on you about this part, Mair. The truth is —"

"Please, Gwilym," she interrupted. "Don't…" She paused, as if to collect herself. He stroked her shoulder. "It's not why I asked you up here, Gwilym," she said. She tossed her hair, her face momentarily disturbed, then once more a calm enigma. After a moment she gave him a frank gaze. "I'm going to get out of this tight dress."

She stood up. Then, as if on impulse, she took his hands in hers and pulled him to his feet. She brushed her lips against his face in a series of quick kisses. Clasping her to him, his cheek against hers, he murmured how beautiful she was and how much he wanted her, feeling her breasts press against the thin material of his shirt as she breathed. Over his shoulder she observed both hands of the clock approaching the figure eleven. She clasped him still more tightly, then suddenly pushed him away: "I've just got to get out of this dress." She touched his arm a moment, lingeringly, then turned and walked into the bedroom, casting a last, earnest look over her shoulder.

He followed her.

"Unzip me, will you?"

Moments later she was on her back, cooperating as he removed her underwear. His wet mouth slithered over her. He kneaded and stroked her breasts and inserted his fingers into her vagina. He sucked her breasts and then massaged her clitoris with his tongue while she

111

gazed at the orange street light on the patterned curtains, thinking how Gethin's hours of work made sex a rarity. Gethin said that asleep she looked so calm it made his heart stand still. She loved Gethin, even though he lacked what it took in the hard world. Gwilym Llywelyn faced around and kissed her again so that she tasted her own fluids. He penetrated her and she ran her fingernails up and down his spine giving small gasps. A new sound made by the cars in the night below told her it had started raining. He turned her and raised her buttocks to mount her from behind, his hands grasping her hips. Her body began to sense a climax it would not achieve. At the appropriate moment she faked an orgasm.

They lay still, he clasping her to him. She had not been unfaithful in the conjugal bed before and was surprised by how lonely it made her feel. She moaned his name, knowing he would soon start thinking of leaving. She turned her body and kissed him on the mouth pressing her wet vagina against his thigh. She cupped his balls in her right hand while the fingers of her left intertwined with his hair.

"Tell me," she murmured. He pressed himself tight against her. "Tell me," she whispered.

"What?"

Assuming a little child's voice she begged tearfully, playfully: "Oh, tell me."

He was amused.

"Tell you what, my love?"

"Tell me, now, tell me."

It dawned on him.

"Oh! Well… Hefina Parry is up for a small part in that series I mentioned, which is why I've perhaps been a bit shy about it tonight. You know her connections. It's going to be a bit awkward. This is confidential, by the way. It's a colourless part, hard to do much with, so I thought of you. You could rescue it, and it's my decision at the end of the day, whatever anyone says." He paused. She waited. So did he. But she asked no further questions. Eventually he felt forced to continue. "The fact is you're much better for it, and I don't think anyone could argue with that. I want you for it, if you decide you want to take it, that is," he added. "It's not a very big part, I'm afraid."

She gave his balls a gentle squeeze.

Leaving the subject, not having told her exactly how small a part it was, he said in a dejected voice: "It hurt when you dropped me, Mair."

"It had got risky, Gwilym."

"We'll have to be very careful this time," he said.

She nuzzled his ear. "Mmm. Tell me more," she murmured.

He told her, this time admitting the part was very small. He got no response. Whatever had made him think she'd take it? Out of work didn't have to mean desperate, did it? After all, her husband was earning. "Wait till you see the script," he begged. "Maybe the part can be extended here and there. With you in it the character may justify it."

She sighed, pretending to be languid, sated, incapable of taking anything in.

Gwilym Llywelyn wanted more reaction than he was getting. He needed to know. "There'll be other parts," he assured her. "But I'd like you to take this one, Mair. Do it just for me, will you? Help me out." He shook her arm for a response. She murmured something sleepily with her eyes shut. It sounded like, "tomorrow".

He left without an answer, blowing a kiss, saying he'd ring.

She sat up in a listening position the minute she heard the front door close. As soon as she heard his car drive off she ran a bath. Naked, she set about changing the sheets. She found she was still wearing her lucky charm. She removed it with mixed feelings but with her heart firmly set against the hairdresser's. Gethin would find her asleep, as usual. Would his heart stand still? Her loneliness returned.

In the bathroom, a questioning ghost observed her from the steamed up mirror.

She wiped the wet mirror with her hand and stared.

"What's so special about you, anyway?" she demanded of it. The changed face in the mirror looked hurt, upsetting her further. "So?" she challenged. "So?"

PURE WELSH

One weekend before the days of political correctness I find myself sitting right in the front at the Royale, as the place was called at that time. When the fat comedian walks on stage he behaves as though he's delighted to see me. In his sports coat and open shirt he looks like anyone else.

If everyone in Africa held hands around the globe, half the black bastards would drown.

Witty, eh?

Someone asked Stevie Wonder what it's like being blind. It could be worse, he said, I could be black as well.

Nice fella, this comedian, rough diamond. Likeable for being a bit tubby.

Hey, you. He points to a young fellow with very short hair. *You look like a nice lad, go and piss on that black.* He points at me, but there's not much laughter. *Plane load of Africans crashed, two hundred killed. Broke my fuckin' heart it did. Six empty seats, there was.*

Yes, really witty material. So, I'm looking around to see who's in the audience and there's this crowd of young farmers there, with a different idea of what immigration is. And it's something the fat comedian knows nothing about.

…watching Swan Lake. It's where the swan is dying, but it's a black swan, so bollocks to it anyway…

He's not getting that much response and this is the moment he moves away from the mike to a small table holding his glass of water.

OK. This is my chance!

I'm up on the stage in a trice wearing a smile with the mike in my hand. The surprise on his face turns quickly into a grin. He lifts his palms towards the ceiling in a gesture of friendly compliance.

I say in Welsh: "I've got to tell you this one, boys."

It's a language the fat comedian doesn't understand one word of.

On my lips it produces a surprised silence. All eyes are upon me.

"This is one for patriots. Any Tregaron boys here?"

Several young farmers raise a shout.

Remember, I'm speaking in Welsh.

"A fat Englishman, like this one behind me, goes into the Red Lion with a parrot on his shoulder. 'Where d'you get that?' asks the barman. 'Where the hell have you been living?' says the parrot, 'there are dozens of 'em moving in every month.'"

Like a swallow to its nest, that one. A second or two to sink in and there's a riot of laughter. The best of it is, it's one of the fat comedian's own jokes turned around!

My arm is gripped. Something is said in my ear. The microphone is wrenched from my hand and it's back with me to my seat.

"Sssssssss," hiss my new friends. "Boo," they shout. Things begin to look black for the fat comedian, if I'm allowed that pun.

"Bravo," he grins from the stage, gesturing as if we are colleagues.

This is a famous comedian. He gets given time on television.

I'm on my feet.

"Well, boys, whose side are you on?" I shout in Welsh.

They yell their support. The place is in uproar.

Then, before worse can happen, I'm between two large fellas heading towards the door with my feet not touching the ground.

"Come on, boys," I say to them sweetly, in English, "play the white man."

"Sorry mate," says one of them, as they put me out. He means it, too. He doesn't like what he's had to do. That's his problem. My problem is, I'm outside. Inside, the young farmers strike up a patriotic song about how the town square isn't big enough for their boys – I mean, our boys, don't I?

When Gwenda my girlfriend comes out after me, I am astonished. She hadn't accompanied me and I hadn't mentioned my intention of going there. Walking down Eastgate I have little to say and Gwenda shows she knows when to keep quiet. I am thinking things to myself. In my opinion, the fact that the Welsh should tolerate that comedian, let alone invite him to perform, shows how completely this nation has forgotten the Blue Books. These days, those who protest against our language dying forget bigger causes. *Ni wyr y gog ond un ungainc:* the cuckoo only knows one tune.

Who am I?

Does it matter? I am one of *you.*

I let go of Gwenda's hand. I am glad of my Welsh background, glad of my nationality and glad of her. I'm glad of everything I've got because what would I have otherwise? But right now I feel more comfortable apart.

"Don't react personally," she says, taking my hand again. "You made a big hit. You had a real effect. They'll always remember it. So will that bloody comedian."

I make no reply.

"You won hearts and minds," she insisted. "You acted politically."

It's a distinction she always makes, as if politics is a cool affair and nothing like the turmoil I feel.

All I can say is that I'll piss on the fat bastard's grave one day if I can find it, whether that's a political act or not.

Will political correctness cure this Britain we live in? Gwenda is a believer, and I suppose that fighting the good fight is better than being cynical or just out for a good time, as most are these days. Personally, I'm not convinced that we are all united beneath the skin by the good side of our humanity, but I'll still side with Gwenda and those who think that way, right or wrong. Doubt doesn't help. Better to try and believe the world will be saved by the few.

Friday night in Aberystwyth. The streets are full of young people under the streetlights and the staring moon, calling out and laughing as they wander from pub to pub. They are all – *we* are all – so similar in our dress, our desires and ambitions. Perhaps complete similarity is the answer, becoming closer and closer neighbours in the global village. But there are beggars with blankets, too, drinking cans of Special Brew in the doorways of Smiths and the Spar. Their dogs sprawl at their feet. Where did they come from? Who are they?

"I hope you're not going to make a habit of nights like tonight," says Gwenda, squeezing my hand.

Everything makes sense to Gwenda. I think she actually has reasonable feelings.

We met at some forgettable performance in the Arts Centre some six months ago, a girl with the Welsh of Ysgol Glantaf and a black *Gog* whose Welsh is stronger than his English. Of course, Gwenda comes from the only Welsh city with a large black population. How many Welsh people think of these Cardiff citizens as Welsh at all? Her grandparents were Italian. It shows just a bit in her colouring and in her hair and black eyes. Gwenda Brachi, my dark, Italian beauty. Her grandfather, Antonio, sold ice-cream in Morriston and learned Welsh, while another arm of the Brachis settled in Swansea, another in Llanelli – long journeys in those days in vehicles called charabancs. Her family got absorbed in just one generation. Welsh is weakening everywhere now, but this granddaughter is taking a degree in it and is a member of the Welsh Language Society, and is walking through Aberystwyth hand in hand with a black Welshman. Is this progress?

We turn into North Parade, which is quiet, having no pubs. Tall Victorian houses look down calmly on the broad street. They are nearly all commercial by now, shops, surgeries, chemists, restaurants, hotels, flats, bedsits. They are no longer the residences of well-to-do families with servants.

"I hadn't planned on seeing you tonight," I say.

"You don't say," she mocks.

"How did you know I'd be there?"

"I guessed."

"Hell, how?"

"I know you."

She may actually understand me. That's more than I can say for myself.

I stay silent.

At the end of North Parade we turn left into Queens Road and walk towards the Crystal Palace Hotel.

"Did you consider what could have happened?" I ask.

She gives me a glance.

I say: "It could have got nasty."

She's wearing jeans and leather, not much make-up. She opens her handbag and takes out half a brick which she sets down by the side of the road. We walk on without a word.

It is so crowded in the Crystal Palace you can scarcely move.

Waiting to get served at the bar, my feelings are a difficult matter. Gwenda is too mature for bravado. She was with me all the way. How many men are that lucky? Yet, still, I'm afraid to let her too near me, afraid of feelings. Feelings are the problem. Distance continually proves its worth. Why invite trouble when you can't change anything, my father asks me. Why not just take what life offers? But I can't seem to heed him. He isn't volatile like me. He says it's pointless carrying a grudge against experience. Relegate, he says. Walk away with contempt, but don't go looking for trouble. You need to learn to relax.

My father has a quiet place inside himself where he can go anytime, but I have no such resort. Peace of mind is a knack that evades me.

Just tell yourself that the past has happened and there's nothing you can do about it, advised my father, walking in the countryside behind our house, when I was about to leave home for the first time. That's the attitude to adopt, he stressed. The rest will follow. Look around you, look at these mountains. Take them in. Let them possess you. Then you'll find you take them with you. Remember that *now* is what you're getting through, and that sometimes it's wonderful.

Now this drunken girl at the bar with long blond hair and enormous spectacles wants to show she loves me better than all the other dolls in the Crystal Palace toy box. She is drunk and talking too much and unexpectedly finds herself troubled by how often the word 'black' crops up metaphorically in ordinary speech. The word 'white' can mean 'blessed' in Welsh and the connotations of 'black' need hardly be gone into. Drink makes her suddenly over-sensitive to these reflections in the mirror of language and in the end she is silenced, abashed. It's embarrassing, not easy to ignore. It's real. It's not easy to explain. She takes my hand and places it on her breast. With her other hand she touches my face. This puts us in a new arena of some ambiguity. The juke-box is playing *Hotel California*, "…this can be Heaven and this can be Hell…"

"Where do you come from?" she asks.

I tell her.

"That's close to me," she says.

"I can tell," I say, and rejoin Gwenda.

Soon it is not far off closing time.

In the taxi home Gwenda falls into animated conversation with the driver, first in English, then in Irish, which she learns as part of her Celtic Studies. Every Irishman seems to speak a little of his own language, and is proud of it. I wish it were true of the Welsh. I love the Welsh language as my own first language, and it also protects me from prejudice from other Welsh-speakers. Too few to afford divisions, we always kick off on the right foot.

As I relax in the back of the taxi, Goldilocks churns around in my mind along with the racist comedian and young farmers, swirling among the drunken students in the pub and the new rough sleepers in shop doorways with their blankets and alcohol, and to replace all of it equations come into my mind, true and calm, better than the words of any language. My PhD is in astro-physics and I work hard to succeed. If I chose to worship anything, to humble myself before anything, it would not be God. It would be the beckoning of mathematics. That is my quiet place. An image of my father appears. He is on the other side of a railway carriage window, running briefly alongside my train, full of pride, seeing his son off to university, twenty years a clerk in the dole office without promotion. Not me, though, I say to myself. Times have changed. I'm going to be *somebody*, however hard I have to work. But suddenly I'm in a café, the meaningless writing of rain on the window, catching snatches of a joke about Rasta and Liza from another table, and then hearing silence, my presence noticed.

I phoned home last night.

We chatted about the family, a factory cutting its workforce, a quarry reopening after a century. I could tell something was the matter. I could almost see the grooves that appear between my father's cheeks and chin when he's upset but not showing it.

"And the bowls team?"

"Playing Llan on the weekend for the cup."

"Fingers crossed then. How are things at work?"

"Fine."

"Anything new?"

He confessed something small had happened at school, upsetting Meinir, my little sister. "Thoughtless words on the playground. You know how children can be."

"Children can be cruel."

"It was only a small thing."

"She'll forget," I comforted him.

We both knew it was a lie. As the saying has it: *Peth garw yw cof plentyn*: A child's memory is a harsh thing.

Foolish Gwenda has brought up the question of Northern Ireland and our young taxi driver has become silent. His political feelings are his business. He's from a border town, the name of which I've already forgotten. He's as distant, suddenly, as his passenger in the back seat.

Words are what did it.

"Thoughtless words," my father said.

ALWAYS THE LOVE OF SOMEONE

After breakfast Pritchard sat amid the long windows of the sun lounge flicking through a copy of *Hello* magazine he'd picked up at Heathrow some days before. The room had a yellow carpet and a row of white lampshades. A long mirror sidled up against the doorjamb in which those departing passed themselves, maybe glimpsing those who watched them. Outside, a melancholy promenade followed an empty shoreline.

A few guests drifted in and out. An Asian woman with beautiful, aquiline features entered and departed again, a woman slender enough to look tall when she wasn't. She was dressed in white slacks and a blue top that did nothing for her, but she didn't need anything done for her. She looked about the same age but more beautiful than Najma, with whom Pritchard had made love oh, God, when? All those years ago back in Cardiff. He'd been the younger partner then, in a world where John Travolta was a dancer and the microchip was a baby and banks had a lot more clerks. The woman departed leaving an impression of repose and poise. Pritchard stared after her retreating bottom. He was developing a thing about repose, to the extent of trying out relaxation techniques. He'd always had a thing about bottoms.

He'd come here to relax and reflect. On what, he wasn't sure, but of late his mind had been turning to the notion of value, which had somehow got to do with brand names. Not that Pritchard didn't always buy the best brands. But when you'd made your pile and enjoyed what there was to enjoy and weren't getting any younger, well, life presented a bit of a challenge. Pritchard found himself looking for direction, improvement even. But good resolutions, if contemplated, needed something to make them stick, something certain enough to swear by.

What had she seen, that beautiful Indian woman? No doubt a tall, middle-aged man looking at a magazine as if it were a puzzle. Pritchard knew he was beginning to lose the physical magnetism he'd relied on all his life. She'd hardly given him a glance. Of course, she was doubtless more used to getting attention than giving it. The New Year celebrations had provided a dance, during which guests had got to know each other, but she had not attended. Maybe she had just arrived.

It was too early in the year to sit outside. The sky was blue, but the day wouldn't warm up till later. This was not a well-known winter resort and Pritchard was glad he'd discovered it, as it was quiet. That summer he'd found the English at St Tropez shallow. Pritchard had out-Englished the English since he'd crossed the bridge when he was twenty, a bridge over more than the Severn and maybe hard to recross when you met with success, he conjectured. Here in this resort it was restful. Pritchard needed a rest from a high position with a Building Society that had turned into a Bank. Although he had decided on a backward step from London to a job in Reading, and had recently moved to the quiet, dormer village of Sonning, he still needed a rest from his successful hobby as a speculator, shorting shares and trading futures. Few knew about this hobby and his wealth. Not that Pritchard was miserly or avaricious, far from it. No, any man would understand how three divorces taught you to keep such things close to your chest.

Fewer women close to his chest might have brought less tribulation and fewer forks in his road, and now, on top of it all, there was this blunt whisper of age saying, 'You're going to die,' till it dawned on you that finding an attitude towards death had something to do with your attitude towards life, including your attitude towards the person you lived with. It needed working out.

Pritchard had always been willing to learn. He'd learned as much as he had so far, he felt, because he had a big heart. He had never meant to hurt anyone. At the end of the day he was a normal guy at an age when a man starts to question what has brought him to where he is. And the answer, as far as he could see, was love. He had genuinely kept on falling in love. And, unfortunately, the women had, too. It was always the love of someone that had brought him trouble. Pritchard had loved too much. But could love really be the wicked fairy at the feast? He had worshipped some of those women. Danielle, for example, who had introduced him to photography. They'd spent half their time in a darkroom. With wispy Fiona it had been poetry, which Pritchard still liked to read, and to this day Fiona sent him poetry. Sporty, long-legged Lucy had taught him how to sail. How could he regret any of it?

Until now, Pritchard had enjoyed his memories, but recently there were too many women rising up in the nights out of the valleys of Toss and Turn, blaming him for leaving them, even for meeting them. With their individual gestures and expressions they laid his poor conscience to siege. Yet why blame him and not the fate that flicks the unexpected encounter into the dreary day? It was a sad fact that happiness always comes at someone else's expense. Pritchard looked at the white lampshades in the sun lounge and shrugged, *C'est la vie.* This led him to reflect on the benefits of fidelity and trust, the protection it offered from the tyranny of love. He pondered this with warm feelings towards the new soul mate that had helped him develop his new thoughtfulness, his nature-loving fourth wife left behind in England, who was delighted by how he'd embraced her passion for flora. Pritchard had already committed to memory quite a list of peaceful plants.

The only fly in the ointment was his wife's job with a London agency, which she refused to give up and which had condemned him to his lonely holiday. But every cloud has a silver lining. Being alone enabled Pritchard to reflect on a particular phenomenon of womanhood, of which he had always been aware but had noticed anew in the women staying at this hotel. It had to do with the calm, immobile expressions their faces assumed when they sat alone.

It was not a quietude evident in very young women, he'd noticed, and Pritchard tended not to look at old ones. But the slightly older ones, young enough to be beautiful, the ones Pritchard always looked at these days, in these he suspected a kind of stasis, a stratum of mental inactivity. It made him think of a park early on a fine morning. He had scrutinized their faces to see if it were an effect of make-up, an illusion, but it was not. It was genuine vacancy, he decided, a state of awaiting, something very different from the quiet moments of men, who sighed and grunted in repose as if it were a form of imprisonment. The stillness of these women touched Pritchard like light from a keyhole in the night. It made him wonder what tranquil refuge lay within. Perhaps it explained how they could cope with so many different things at once. Maybe it had something to do with an attitude towards time. Women were good at waiting. They waited nine months to give birth. Pritchard had ceased to be surprised by the things women could do.

In these easily interrupted trances women were quite aware of the here-and-now, quite alert when you approached them, as the charming Pritchard had indeed done in the case of those that spoke English. He had asked what they'd had in their minds during those still moments, begging an honest reply on grounds of being a portrait painter. But his interviews had left him none the wiser. So, was this female haven something he merely imagined, or something too common and ordinary to convey, something shared by all creatures, perhaps, except male humans? Pritchard felt he was seeing something important, but what it was he saw, he could not find out. He phoned friends who might help. Lucy told him to think of a spinnaker on a still day. Danielle spoke of the essence of a photograph and the vanished moment. Fiona quoted a line about 'the still centre of the turning world'.

What must it be like, he wondered. Not orderly or purposeful, he was sure. He tried to imagine unorganised perception, a collage of thoughts and feelings, shapes and colours, a soul's eye view. Maybe your soul was one of God's billion eyes. Pritchard dreamed on in the sun lounge, letting himself drift on a slow river of passing time which with luck might carry him, he hoped, like those women, to the essence of the vanishing moment, a peaceful, unthinking sea where motionless winds filled spinnakers at the still centre of the turning world. It didn't happen. His thoughts were soon swimming about again like fish in the bowl of his brain. Disappointment. Nonetheless, Pritchard felt certain his eyes had been opened to something. If only they could be opened a little more.

Soon they would be.

He came to himself as he heard the plop of his magazine striking the floor. He picked it up and put it on the table next to him. A little afterwards he stood up and left the sun lounge.

★ ★ ★ ★ ★ ★ ★ ★ ★ ★

Pritchard discharged into a pristine lavatory, plucked a hair from a nostril and selected for his morning walk a slate-blue jacket and light grey slacks.

Remembering his magazine, he turned into the sun lounge, and there he found the Asian woman. She was sitting like a graven image near the door with her head tilted slightly downward, her eyes half shut.

She wore a white dress and a white cardigan lay over the arm of her chair. Her black hair gleamed on her shoulders. Her feet were clad in white sandals with slender heels. Small, ruby earrings hung from her lobes. These and the gold chain on her throat revealed how shallow was her breathing. Lustre haunted the half closed eyelids. Her hands lay peacefully in her lap. It was as if she had appeared there in his absence like some species of fast growing flower. Pritchard must have stood staring at her for a full minute or more before the eyelids flickered and then rose very slowly as if hauled up by tiny winches. The fascinated Pritchard found two charcoal pupils gazing at him.

"I'm sorry I woke you," he smiled, raising his arms as if at a loss as to what else he could have done.

Lips, pink with pastel lipstick, parted beneath features still placid.

"I wasn't asleep."

The voice, an unexpected contralto, spoke with an English accent.

"I thought you might have been enjoying a doze after that marvellous breakfast."

Her brow wrinkled. Lethargically, she rearranged herself in her chair. "I don't, usually. But I couldn't eat the food on the plane."

Conscious of standing over her, Pritchard took a seat. He leaned forward, meeting those dark eyes. "I hope you will forgive me for staring like that," he said, producing his most charming smile, "but you looked so still just now it seemed almost deliberate. Do you mind if I ask what was in your mind?"

"I was trying to keep it empty."

"Deliberately?"

She nodded.

"I'm interested, you see, because I learned some relaxation exercises recently."

A look of enquiry sharpened her beauty.

He explained: "You concentrate on parts of your body, making a foot feel heavy, or a knee hot." He waved a hand dismissively, gave a laugh. "Sounds crazy, but actually it works."

"Sounds like a sort of meditation. What you just caught me doing," she said.

As Pritchard absorbed this intriguing remark his élan deserted him like summer mist and he fell to questioning the woman eagerly. She had been brought up a Hindu, he extracted. "It doesn't necessarily involve meditation," she said, "but as you say, it's relaxing." She regarded his intent expression with a quizzical smile. "Have you been here long? It seems very quiet."

"Three days, and it's very quiet indeed. Hindus believe in reincarnation, don't they?"

She turned her eyes to the window, replying indifferently: "Hindus, Australian aborigines, a few billion living Buddhists, an unknown number of Americans…" Sunlight from outside ridged her cheekbones. She tossed her hair, inscrutable, Aztec-looking.

"I don't know whether I'd like it to be true or not," Pritchard said, with a wistful sigh.

"Well," she said, rekindling good humour with a chuckle, "some used to say an angel makes your soul forget its previous life by touching its nose and squeezing the upper lip." She pointed with a long, gleaming nail. "Your lip does bear the mark of it." Pritchard was too busy imagining the dirty trick pulled on that poor, hypnotised soul to join in with her laughter. He knew about laughter, of course, how infectious it was, and knew full well how a serious conversation put the Rio Grande between two bodies. But he couldn't help himself. This was a new, pilgrim Pritchard on the trail of something he already felt to be hidden like a rune in this hotel, and this was the closest he'd got.

"How could I learn to meditate?"

She shrugged. "Locate a group. Try the internet."

"Will you tell me how it works?"

"You concentrate on an object or a meaningless sound and try and empty your mind, that's all it is."

She saw how intently he listened.

"What's the purpose of it in your religion?" he asked.

She sucked in a disobliging breath. "OK," she conceded. "Think of consciousness as a river, the water always changing but the river the same. You're trying to see into the river of universal consciousness by switching off your individual mind. If you succeed, you'll know yourself as you also exist within all things. Not exactly modern thinking." Her laughter, showing perfect teeth, winged away from what she had said. Pritchard knew it was time to talk of something else and invite her for a walk, but he didn't feel he could wait.

"Does meditating affect your life?" he asked.

From outside somewhere came the insect harmony of a boys' band. She tossed her hair in an indifferent way. 'She tossed her hair like I wasn't there', he remembered the song putting it, long before this girl's time. She shifted her position and was momentarily off balance, an elbow and a knee jutting, restored to grace with one upward jerk of a young foot. She twisted away, seeking the direction of the music, the top of her back showing an intricately fashioned spine.

"It's supposed to make you lean towards harmony," she muttered, unaccomodatingly.

This intrigued Pritchard.

"What's harmony?"

Her head turned slowly, examining him with a slantwise, suspicious look before her features relapsed into a patient expression. "Universal consciousness is affected by thoughts and actions and returns what we give out. That's called Karma. Harmony is your awareness of this."

"You reap what you sow?"

She threw out a hand, palm upwards, like an empty dish, the movement causing her breast to follow in that dress designed to assist.

"What am I, a guru?"

Pritchard silently cursed himself. He hadn't been attending to her and now he couldn't ask her to come for a walk. He lifted a hand with an appeasing grin. "OK, enough. It was just new to me, that's all. Truly, I'm sorry. No more."

To take the edge off the moment he lowered his eyelids, intending to look up with a self-deprecating chuckle. The moment his eyes closed, however, he found himself thinking how right he had been, even about the river, which he had imagined himself floating on. Longing all the more for the secrets held by this beautiful woman, he opened his eyes.

She was gone.

Pritchard was astounded. Had she turned herself into air? She must have risen from her chair without a squeak or a creak? He wouldn't even see her at breakfast, he remembered. He should have taken control, concentrated on her, not his own curiosity. He should have laughed with her.

Next time they'd get on like bread and jam, he promised himself.

Pritchard enjoyed a challenge. She had made herself alluring, he'd been aware of it, and she was going to find this resort too quiet. He'd find an opportunity. Pritchard's charm knew nothing was irreparable. It would not be difficult.

He stood up, checked his handsome, self-assured figure in the mirror by the door, and set off towards the Reception Desk. As he approached it he palmed a sizeable banknote from his wallet.

"I was just talking to an Indian lady in the sun lounge," he said casually to the receptionist, standing at his ease, his weight to one leg. His right hand moved carelessly across the surface of the counter. "She checked in yesterday. I don't suppose you could look up her name for me, could you? She told me, but I've forgotten."

The receptionist, slim with an undershot jaw, furrowed his brow uncooperatively, but did check the register. After a moment, he said, unsmilingly: "Mrs Jasmin Medhurst."

"Thank you," said Pritchard. The banknote lay between them on the counter. He saw the receptionist's hand twitch. "Perhaps you could help me further," murmured Pritchard.

The man smiled helpfully. "Room 375, sir. She occupies it alone. She is from England. I will write the address for you."

Pritchard reached for the paper the young man proffered.

Good Lord, he thought, for she lived in Chertsey, near Reading. Could Karma do this?

WOULD THAT EVEN BE LUCKY?

Y ou didn't fully realize how beautiful Julia was till you saw her naked. You noticed the eye-catching features and long black hair and leisurely walk in the long skirt, but she wore no make-up and all her clothes were shapeless. Naked, she had big, firm breasts, a narrow waist and long legs without an ounce of fat. She must have had *something* in her wardrobe to show herself off, like every other woman, I thought to myself.

The phone rang.

It would be an unusual time not to be home so I padded downstairs to pick up the handset in the kitchen rather than take the call in the bedroom.

"Just to say we've arrived. It rained all the way down. You know how I hate driving in the rain. Kids were great. They played word-games... we stopped twice for the toilet and a drink... How did your meeting go?" After a while I said, "Actually, Margaret, I haven't got any clothes on. I was in the shower... yes, well, I knew it could be you... no, I'm not sitting on the bed making it wet, I'm in the kitchen. It's warmer. I really don't know, I don't know why I came down here. Yes... of course... yes... Glad you called... Love you, too."

The kitchen clock showed 4.30 p.m. I crossed the room to look out of the window at next-door's house and garden, then poured two pint glasses of orange squash and went back upstairs.

Julia was sitting up, her knees drawn up under the duvet. She had pulled it round her shoulders for warmth and had relit the joint. How long had it been since I'd smoked a joint in bed with a beautiful woman? And this one was probably the most beautiful I'd ever had. I'd taken it all for granted once, youth being wasted on the young. I felt as if fifteen years had fallen away, as if I were a student again.

"How on earth did Iwan find you, if I'm allowed to ask?" I said, getting back into the bed.

We had never talked like this before this situation came about.

There had come a knock at the back door and I had hurriedly put the joint out and done my best to keep her outside, but she sniffed the air and winked, which suggested she was entirely different from what she looked like and what I'd thought. So she came in and we smoked and talked and listened to music and one thing led to another. You know how it is when you're smoking. Then, again, maybe you don't. Anyhow, next thing we knew, with the weed and all, and a few things we felt we had in common, we found ourselves close enough not to leave much point in staying downstairs.

"The internet," she replied.

Of course, I thought. Iwan wouldn't know how to approach a woman in real life, let alone one like this. But then maybe everyone used the internet these days. What the hell did I know? Julia must have used it. But, then, maybe single mothers had less of a field to play and had to get practical.

"He's a good man," she said, but she sounded none too enthusiastic. "Everything is give-and-take," she added. "Well, what isn't? I mean, everything is, isn't it?"

"I suppose," I said, feeling glad my wife loved me and that the kids were mine. "But you could have had anyone you wanted."

"Huh," she said.

"Why, isn't it true? Don't you ever look in the mirror?"

"Most guys are married."

"Well, *you've* certainly made *him* happy."

"What does that mean? Do I strike you as unhappy, then?"

"I didn't say that, but since you mention it... anyway, forget it," I said, taking the joint from her. "I'm being sexist. Didn't mean anything. You've got a good life." Better than most single mothers, is what I didn't say. I often wondered why there were so many of them, but with a very beautiful woman like Julia you were struck by the tragedy of it, the difference between what she had and what she could have ended up with if she'd just played her cards.

I set about rolling another joint. She drank her squash. "This is really good," she said. "Dope makes you so dry."

One night when we were round there and I was talking to Iwan she had chatted to Margaret about her past, with Iwan looking back and fore all the time from me to them. It added up to hard times with two different guys, one dour and the other manic, which I happened to know was true since both were local. This was after having the kid down in London by an artist she split up with, about whom she said nothing. The message was one of good fortune in finding happiness with Iwan. But if you knew Iwan you wouldn't want to imagine how repetitive her life must have been. The reason I had looked out of the window in the kitchen was because the clock told me it was the exact time Iwan should be in his aviary tending to his birds, because Iwan did the same things at exactly the same time every single day. He wasn't in his aviary because he wasn't home, being in Shrewsbury seeing his mother, but that's how routine-bound he was, enough to make you check even when you *knew* he wasn't there.

Personally, I didn't mind the guy. I used to call round and drink a can or two of beer with him and watch football.

"What the hell do you talk about?" Margaret asked. "You can't talk about football all the time."

"That's exactly what we talk about," I said.

Then Julia had moved in.

Most guys' lives would have changed. They would have wanted to be seen with her and would have been willing to do what she wanted sometimes. Could a woman like Julia really want to sit in every night watching TV and never get a baby-sitter? Margaret had offered. "No thanks, love," Iwan had said, before Julia could open her mouth.

"Your kid, Ray, must be around somewhere," I said. "Where is he?"

"Playing computer games at a friend's."

"We'll have to be a bit careful when he gets back."

She nodded and stubbed out the joint, tossing her hair. She took the new joint out of my hands the minute I finished it, passing it back after a couple of draws.

Smiling in an unexpected way, she asked out of the blue: "If you thought happiness was waiting, would you go for it and to hell with the world? Would you risk everything?"

"Like, what kind of happiness, Julia?"

"Well, *love*."

Her eyes had an entreating look.

Shit! Had I misjudged her? She'd seemed so normal, this gorgeous, rather sad woman that I didn't know well who lived with the boring guy next door.

A crow landed in the bedroom window sill, one beady eye regarding us, its presence felt, then it was gone.

I said in a steady, mature voice: "We hardly know each other, Julia."

She broke up at that, her hand waving at me as it helplessly tried to ward off hilarity. I started laughing too. The duvet fell revealing her breasts. Wheezing dizzily with laughter, tears in my eyes, I buried my face between them to stifle mirth. Dope does this. When we finally sobered, she said: "But tell me what you think. I want to know what you really think." She turned her face, looking at me again.

I took a long draw on the joint and shrugged.

"Love?"

She nodded.

"Well, I believe in it," I said. "Half the people I know have got divorced because of it."

"Is there such a thing as love that *lasts*?" she pressed. "That's the question. One that won't go away no matter what, even if there's something bad been?"

"It's a hard question," I said. "It changes with time."

"I mean one that changes but still doesn't change, some of it surviving like the way it started."

"What do you think?" I asked.

"Well, yes. But it didn't work out. Just *thinking* about it, in theory, though, doesn't it come down to asking what the most important thing is? In life, I mean? Something you'd make sacrifices for, take risks for?"

"That could just as well be money," I said.

"So, which makes the best sense of life?"

"Do you have someone in mind?" I asked.

She hesitated. "There's someone who's always in my mind." She looked at me as if for an answer to something I understood.

I shrugged. "I don't know if you can even call that lucky."

"No," she said. "What else is there, though?"

Her expression wanted an answer. "Yeah, I know," I said. "There's just the routine of every day. Some comforts, maybe. The occasional bit of fun, like now."

"Yes. Piff!" she said, which I didn't find very flattering.

"Comfort in a nice semi in a decent spot for your Ray to grow up in," I added. "There's always realism, Julia. Iwan's not a bad role model. You're not giving me enough of the duvet." I tugged at it. She tugged it back and a noisy struggle ensued, till our laughter stopped suddenly at the sound of kids outside. We waited. We heard Iwan's front door slam and young voices disappearing down the street.

"Think they heard?" I whispered.

"No. They wouldn't know it was me, anyway."

"They'd know it was me, though, and that Margaret's away. They might even clock you're not around."

She shrugged.

"You're a bit laid back about it, I must say, Julia?"

"Pass the joint."

She took a draw and suddenly started telling me about this first guy she'd lived with, the artist who'd dumped her. Only she kept switching back into the present as she talked. The guy's name was Raymond.

"We had this little flat in a dump of a house between Deptford and New Cross. Rough area. We were always talking about the places we wanted to go, and what we'd do. We spent our spare time in museums and galleries and parks. We didn't have much money. I was nineteen. He was an art student, a sculptor." She turned to me: "A real sculptor. Not like these con artists. He was good looking, too. I could hardly believe he'd picked me. I don't know how many likenesses he carved of me. They were so beautiful, and I don't have even one of them. We sold them for whatever we could get at the end. I sometimes wonder what happened to them all. Whenever I see carvings in antique shops and junk shops I look in case one of them is me. He says we're all isolated – "

"Hold on Julia, you just said he '*says*'."

"We still talk."

She fell silent.

137

"What else does he say?"

"All sorts. He thinks work and community have become meaningless and people are cut off from each other and don't contribute to each other's lives – "

"Lonely consumers, Julia. Get back to the love bit. Do you still sleep with him?" She didn't answer. "You needn't worry, love, I'm not the jealous type," I joked, feeling jealous nonetheless. "Go back to what happened in London."

I began to wonder if I shouldn't have interrupted and if she was going to say anymore, but she was just thinking. After a while she went on.

"I don't know how to begin. I don't know how to describe it. It was as if I had just learned to see. That's what love does. I don't know if you can understand this, but it was like the world breaking free, coming into your eyes like in a 3D film, only for real. Vivid, wonderful reality! Every day I was living with the uniqueness of everything. All because of him! And he talked and talked – to *me*. Me. Someone without much education. He talked about literature, art, politics, history, everything. Something new every day. I felt so happy and honoured to be with him. I felt I could never, ever meet anyone better. The very thought of someone else would have been impossible. It still seems that way. I couldn't imagine ever wanting anyone else. I used to wonder why on earth he'd picked me, with so little in my head to contribute."

I imagined Julia at nineteen and laughed.

She looked at me.

"It's pretty obvious to me, Julia." I said.

"Oh, don't be a fool. A man can find any woman boring, or has that never happened to you? And it cuts both ways. But we weren't ever bored with each other. That would have been inconceivable. We were so wrapped up in each other we could lie in bed together for hours in daytime without even the radio. We could be so childish, then so serious. Ha! We had such plans. None of them ever involved making any money. Little Ray's got his features, you know, as well as his name. And Raymond is in the money now, I'm pretty sure, in 'design'. Doesn't talk much about it 'cause he's bored by it, but he talks to me about what he sculpts. He gets the odd commission, but it hardly pays. He says he's happy. He's more like the Raymond I used to know, again. And he's generous to us." She looked at me. "Iwan..." She tailed off.

I put my arm around her shoulder.

"You've got me wondering all over again about you and Iwan."

I took the joint from her and relit it. She sipped what was left of my squash.

"So, go on," I said. "What happened to the two of you?"

She shrugged. "Little Ray happened, and no money. It had to be either sculpting or his family, us, I mean. But he never stopped sculpting. He wouldn't, or just couldn't. I don't know which."

"And?"

She shrugged. "It just fell apart."

"Why? Because of his addiction to sculpting or lack of money?" I didn't really know why I asked this. I think I wanted to know if art could be stronger than love. "Which was it, do you think?"

She turned and looked at me: "I mean, what the hell is the difference?"

I'd thought I'd seen a difference. I shrugged.

She said: "Pass the joint."

I passed it and set about rolling another, knowing I wasn't going to get that one back, while she went back to telling me what it was she had to tell.

"He sculpted late at night, or sometimes read text books, stopping when the baby cried. Then, before he could get much sleep, it would be time for him to go to work. He delivered papers in the early morning and worked in pubs in the evenings. In between he went into college. But he still fell behind with his course. 'This isn't going to work,' I said to him. He just drove himself on. 'We can't go on like this,' I said. 'We need money, and to make time for things.' But he had switched off. He became like a machine, hardly talking, forcing himself on. We didn't do anything together anymore. We didn't even see that much of each other. One evening, when we'd eaten, I shouted at him. I repeated over and over again without letting up: 'You are going to have to choose.' He got up in the end and went into the bedroom. A little later I heard him sobbing.

"Well, he didn't stop sobbing. Not for a long time. I waited, sitting by him, but he didn't stop sobbing or act like I was there at all. I had to see to the baby, as well. The baby kept crying because he was crying. I had to get the cot into the living room for the baby to sleep. When eventually he did stop sobbing, I went into the bedroom and found him just sitting in a chair, staring. He sat there like one of his own carvings. Hours went by. No one in that house had a phone. There were no mobiles back then. There wasn't a payphone for miles that wasn't vandalized and it was a dangerous area for a girl at night. I've often wondered if things might have turned out different if I'd gone for help, but I had to think of what might happen to the baby if something happened to me, and anyway I didn't want to leave the baby with him the way he was. So I didn't go out. I just waited and waited. When the time came for his paper round he got to his feet and walked out. So nothing was done that time. Things just carried on for another couple of months."

She shrugged.

"And?"

"He ended up with his parents, a real mess. I ended up with my mother. Eventually, he went back to college. He just carried on."

She fell silent.

"Go on."

"There's no more," she sighed. "Life turned into what it is now. He did provide. However little it was, the envelopes came. He never forgot a birthday. His parents helped, but they didn't have much. I used to travel with little Ray to visit them, mainly for a rest. He and I slept together sometimes, but I couldn't reach him. I didn't know what he thought or felt. His parents said it wasn't just with me."

She shrugged again.

"In the end we found other partners. His parents were sorry when that happened. No one stuck with him for long, and as for me, I ended up with Winston up the road, as you know. He was on lithium prescriptions. Gave me a few backhanders, I can tell you, though he. was always sorry afterwards and at least he didn't mind if I talked to Raymond, not like Iwan. At least with Winston the phone might ring and there'd be Raymond, and Winston would usually be good enough to leave the room. But now Raymond has to text me. We have to arrange to talk. I don't even show Iwan I've got a mobile. I mean, doesn't little Ray have a right to talk to his father? You can't just cut someone else's ties. So I ask myself where really it can go, with Iwan and me." She paused. "My mother's arthritis is really bad, now. You've seen her. Well, I sent Raymond this video of little Ray with his gran – this is about a month ago – and he's texting me straight away to ring him and then he's saying, 'Why didn't you tell me your mother was so bad? What's got into you Julia?' He jumps in his car and drives all the way to Hereford to see my mother, though he hasn't seen *me* in weeks." She paused again. "God knows," she sighed. "We're hardly the same people anymore, yet here we are in such a situation. He wants me back."

She gave a sigh.

"Well, that's the whole story. Not much of a one, I suppose. Not one I can say I understand."

"It's a moving story," I said, giving her shoulder a squeeze. "Why don't you just bite the bullet and tell Iwan? The guy is the kid's legal father, after all. He has rights. You do, too. It's only fair."

"You don't know Iwan."

"What do you mean? He's not violent, is he?"

"He's very set about things," she said. "It's hard to live with."

"How hard have you tried to open his eyes? How much have you told him?"

"Not much."

"He's not that unreasonable a guy, Julia."

"Maybe I don't want any concessions from him right now."

That didn't sound very promising for Iwan.

I said: "That was a wonderful story, Julia, a genuine love story. Do you talk to this guy often, like several times a week?"

"Yes."

I asked: "Is he married?"

"That's just it. He's getting divorced."

Ah, I thought, as it all fell into place.

"A genuine love story," I said again. "Usually, they are best left in the past. There's the way you told it, though. Kind of without an ending."

"Exactly. It didn't end. It won't. It just doesn't."

She was looking at me, as if waiting for me to say something more, though I could hardly think what.

I would normally have said that ending it lay in her hands, and was usually a wise thing, because you could jump out of the pan into the fire and end up the same as before except with someone else's kids and a barrel of regrets. But I kept my mouth shut and didn't say anything.

"The past stands in our way," she said, eventually. "He failed us before."

"You say he has no financial problems, now," I reminded her.

Why the hell did I say that?

She gave me a smile, then shrugged, looking sad again. "He could have found a job," she said. "He could have gone back to college later. His love failed me and I've had no kind of life because of that. It's put a gulf between us. I've blamed him for it. And how can he ever make up for it?" She turned and looked at me. "On the plus side, what does blame amount to if love is stronger?"

"Normally, Julia, that's something people never want to see put to the test," I said, thinking of Margaret. "Tell me more about Iwan. Is it because of him you dress like one of the homeless, a fantastic-looking woman like you?"

"Thank you," she said, with heavy irony.

I said: "It's the one thing I'd really like to know, Julia. It's something that bugs me not to understand. Why you dress the way you do, I mean. I'm hardly going to gossip, am I? So tell me."

"Well, since you're so curious about it, Iwan doesn't like men looking at me. It's one of the things he's adamant about."

"One of the things? There are others?"

"Quite a few. Look, I'd rather we dropped it. He's not that bad a guy, and nobody's perfect, and it isn't as if you and I…" She trailed off.

"No," I agreed.

A gust of wind blew an unexpected shower against the bedroom window. Next thing it was raining hard.

"Shit," she said. "Those kids will be back any minute."

I put my hand on her thigh to detain her, saying it was worth waiting a moment to see if it slackened off, but it was too late. She had thrown the duvet back and swung her long legs out of the bed.

Unhurriedly, she picked up her underwear from where it lay on the carpet and put it on. It was like watching one of those cool French films in which a beautiful and unique-looking woman's intentions escape you because they are someone else's life, and you just stare with disconnected wonderment at her bared and desirable existence. The genius of such moments is that you are not there, or are just like an object with eyes, watching a desirable embodiment of what you cannot hope to know, and nothing seems purer. Sex makes not one iota of difference. Add more knowledge, add complications; the magic flees, and the reality maybe hurts. Was it right, what she'd said about life, about love being the only meaning? Was it right about reality in 3D? She'd got me believing, got me to the verge of giving advice that went across the grain with me. I'll never really know, though. I guess you need first-hand experience, and, as I said, would that even be lucky?

No kiss, just the flash of a disappearing smile.

Iwan went half-crazy when she left. I never said a word.

NOTHING IS HAPPENING
BECAUSE THERE'S A POINT

Can it be a love story with no obstacles? That's the question raised by love stories.

I'll have to leave you to decide.

I found her sitting on a bench where the river was widest, silver ripples round an old pram and overhanging trees with new leaves shouting yes. Closest thing to a beauty spot we had in our valley.

It was Sunday. I was down for the weekend and taking a walk to work up an appetite for lunch.

"Hello, Nia."

"Hi, Gavin. Still in Aberystwyth?"

"Yes, looking for a job."

"I'm nursing there, you know. Just started."

"Oh, aye? Maybe we should meet for a drink. Catch up on things."

A small gold chain rose and fell in the V inside her blouse. She had black hair and dark eyes and looked demure, which she certainly wasn't. Her parents never knew how she used to get changed at a friend's on Saturday nights into the shortest skirts you ever saw. She'd been a couple of years ahead of me at school, but maybe that didn't matter now. I joined her on the bench.

"Still getting bashed up on demos?" she asked.

"Where've you been living, Nia, down a mine? There aren't any, any more. No, I'm a lamb these days."

"My dad always says steer clear of people setting the world to rights."

Her dad worked in the DVLA in Swansea, kept to himself and never said boo to a goose.

"Aye, but he's got a soft spot for me, your dad."

"Oh, has he, now? And how would you know, may I ask?"

"I'm an artist, Nia. I can sense things." Leaning so that our heads

145

were close, I pointed at her parents' house, visible behind an old bike someone had thrown in the river. "Back there, you said something like: 'How long will dinner be? I think I'll go for a stroll by the river,' and now there's your dad in the window, look. He doesn't mind you sitting with me at all. He looks pleased."

"Built in binoculars you got, is it, Gavin Griffiths?"

"Sensitive vision. I can see his lips moving, Nia. I can see what he's saying. Well, good God! Knock me down with a feather! Who'd have thought he'd say that?" I gave an astonished look.

She grinned. "Aye, aye. Go on, then, what?"

"He said: 'She's talking to that Gavin Griffiths. Goodness, he's putting an arm round her shoulder. She could put him on the right road, our Nia. Lovely boy, at heart. I hope something comes of it.' Bloody hell, Nia! Isn't that good news?"

She burst out laughing.

Nia's laughter had been famous at school, a line of Chopin off the rails.

"Gerraway with you," she said. Then she looked at her watch. "I must get back. It's a crime to be late for dinner in our house."

We stood up together, separate ways to go. We dawdled.

"Well," she said.

"Well…"

I felt shy now I wasn't putting on my chat-up act. She knew me well enough.

She smiled, and waited, bit of a twinkle in her eyes.

"Could I, er, see you, then, Nia? In Aberystwyth?"

She gave me the number of the Nurse's Home where she was staying temporarily. Most people still didn't have mobiles back in the early 'nineties.

My mother served dinner as soon as I got in.

"Where did you go, then? Meet anyone?"

I told her.

"Who did he say? Hollands?"

"Rowlands," said my father.

"He must be talking about Heulwen Rowlands' daughter. Does this girl's mother work in the Spar?"

"Hell, I don't know."

"What else do you know about her, then?"

"Nothing much. She's a nurse."

"That's right, too. Must be Heulwen's daughter. At least she's a local girl. Not a bad family."

"Hey, steady on," I said. "We only talked."

I busied myself with a roast potato.

"Takes after her mam, I hear," said my mother. "You ought to see that Heulwen out at a do."

"Aye, I remember," chuckled my father.

"But I thought she had a boyfriend, that one," my mother said.

Next morning the coach left town for open country, then a brief whiz up the M4 to Carmarthen before crawling North for a couple of hours.

I got off in Aberystwyth.

★ ★ ★ ★ ★ ★ ★ ★ ★

I rang Nia from payphones and left messages.

She seemed to be always working.

I didn't have money to take her out, anyway. I couldn't afford a girlfriend. I couldn't even afford those phone calls.

I finally got her, early Friday afternoon.

"What have you been doing all week?"

"Working. What have you been up to, Picasso?"

"Reading."

"Reading what?"

"Nigel Lawson's memoirs. *The View from No 11.*"

"Jesus Christ."

We arranged to meet that evening.

Twenty minutes later the doorbell rang and there came a knock on my room door. It was Nia, in jeans and a skimpy top. "So, I'm early, OK? It's a great day. Let's go for a walk, you're only reading. Why are you reading that, anyway?"

"Learning what went wrong."

"Come on, then, Mr Happiness."

We walked up to the golf course and across high fields, descending on to a pebbly beach where we sat watching men fishing.

"So, what are you hoping to learn from Nigel Lawson?"

"Why I can't get a job. And why they set on us the way they did."

"They're talking about privatising coal, too, aren't they?"

I nodded. "Another 30,000 on the dole. Everything comes from abroad, now."

"You still painting?"

"Not much. I mean, where? You saw the size of my room."

"There's outside. You've got the time."

I found myself nodding. "Yeah, I should."

She smiled. "You could paint me."

"I get a good likeness, you know."

"There we are, then. Next time I get a day off."

We took the tourist route back over Constitution Hill where coin telescopes pointed at the Llyn Peninsula across Cardigan Bay. Below lay the pretty holiday town where we lived. I felt so content in Nia's company that I told her so and said I'd like to see more of her. She said she felt the same but had a boyfriend, a teacher in one of the Welsh-language schools in Cardiff.

I stared dumbly.

"It's no good when you're a long way apart," she went on. "It was just a matter of time." She added: "I'll tell him. If you really are interested."

I took this in slowly.

I hadn't even kissed her and she was giving someone up. Things were supposed to take longer.

"Hey, in there," she said, tapping the side of my head and peering at me. "So? You interested in what I said? Well, are you?"

"Course I am."

"All right, that's settled, then, is it?"

"Well, yes, I suppose."

"What do you mean, 'suppose'?"

"OK, ok, it's settled. Look, Nia, it's only fair to tell you that I am totally broke. I can hardly afford a bag of chips. I use teabags twice."

"Never mind that. Are you sure about *me*?"

Well, that was plain enough. Not a moment to show doubt.

"Yes," I said.

"Well, kiss me, then."

I kissed her, but soon we heard people coming.

She jerked her head towards the path.

"Come on, I'm hungry."

We strolled along the prom eating hotdogs, stopping to talk to people we knew, introducing each other. Eventually, we turned vaguely in the direction of my room.

It was the size of my father's shed with just one chair. I put the kettle on and sat next to her on the bed. She put her arm around my waist. Once started, things proceeded much faster than a fellow has a right to hope. When I fumbled with her bra her hands flew behind her back and unclipped it. The kettle switched itself off.

"That was good, the second time," she declared, as we got dressed. "I'm hungry again. I've only had that hotdog all day."

We ate out, fish and chips. Then she went home to change.

She came back all made-up in a tiny black dress.

"What's in here, Gavin?" she asked, opening my wardrobe door.

"Precious little, I'm afraid."

"Still, you may as well put something different on. Go and have a shower. I'll wait here."

That evening she swallowed so much lager I wondered how she fitted into that dress. The pub had a disco. She insisted on dancing oftener than I wanted to. I hadn't been going out much in the evenings and had never been a big drinker. She guided me home under streetlights that seemed loosed from their moorings, put me to bed, and left.

If she had a day off ahead of her, there was no stopping Nia. She'd call round in a body-hugging jumper, fishnet stockings and a skirt the size of a handkerchief, or a T-shirt and tight jeans. You looked at her in apple green earrings, miniskirt to match and a topaz top unzipped half way to her red shoes and you just couldn't picture her dispensing drugs to patients full of tubes.

'Loud'. 'Cheap'. 'Common', I said.

'Hoity-toity'. 'Snob'. 'Bookworm', she retorted. "How old are you?" she'd ask, "twenty-four or fifty-four?"

She liked to mimic the young Welsh farmers who came into town on weekends, picking up slight differences in their accents, making them laugh at each other. They were mostly nationalists. I would be included in their Welsh conversations, but replied in English.

"Speak Welsh," Nia would reprove. "You better talk more of it because if we ever have kids they'll be talking Welsh."

"Kids?" I muttered, bemused.

We'd been going out for a month.

★ ★ ★ ★ ★ ★ ★ ★ ★

I got three hours teaching at the Further Education College, and then I got a bit of part-time clerking as well. I was able to show interest when a friend told me about a cheap basement flat up for rent.

The window drew a mean light from a narrow well below pavement level and the furniture was second-hand when Noah threw it out of the ark. I refused to look at anything dearer and told Nia I was surprised she suggested it. I didn't realise what she had in mind, till she gave notice at the nurses' home. The flat had two rooms, a kitchen, a bathroom and a telephone line and was plenty big enough, and while it may not have been a necessary part of my plan, it did seem natural for us to live together.

Yet why? We'd not been going out long and we were not in the grip of those obsessive longings associated with love.

I have no answer.

Far from being an obstacle, her father took to joining mine for a pint in The Mill back home.

In from work, Nia would lie on the settee in her blue uniform, sip the coffee I'd made for her and fall asleep. Then, just when I'd started tiptoeing around, she'd be shedding clothes on her way to the bathroom. "I'm not on in the morning. Where shall we go? I wanna dance."

"You sure? You looked like shit just now."

"Bet you say that to all the girls."

150

"You need an early night."

"You need exercise. You're putting on weight."

"Why do you get so tired at work?"

"Don't ask. It's bloody frantic. Except for the managers."

We'd go dancing and she'd come alive. She could dance all the possibilities of personality, while I did my rhythmic shuffle. Most of the time I sat and watched, trying not to drink too much. She called me 'Wild Thing'.

She spoke to her mother in a mixture of Welsh and English and I fell into the way of it when I answered the phone, so that it was with her mother that I started speaking Welsh again. When I handed the phone to Nia, she'd go into this routine of talking about me as if I wasn't there. She held the headset away from her ear, since her mother tended to shout down the phone. I could hear every word.

"But he seems just right for you."

"There's where you are wrong, see, Mam. He loses his temper all the time. If he can't find something he starts shouting. No, he's still sitting right here. I don't care if he can hear. Of course he won't like it, but I don't like him shouting, either."

She would look at me while saying such things with a trace of a smile.

"What's the matter with you, girl?"

"Things hard to live with, Mam, like men losing their tempers."

"What are you doing with him then?"

"Be getting rid of him, don't you worry. Next week."

"You bring him home here. I haven't met him properly yet."

When she put the phone down, I started: "Lovely girl, you're not so bloody perfect yourself, you know. I have to step round your dirty knickers and stuff all over the bedroom floor. You never put anything away, so nothing can be found. No wonder I lose my temper now and again. If the bedroom was clearer I might be able to do some painting in it. You don't put lights out after you, either, nor shut doors. Yes, hmm. Sorry to be so plain."

"Best way, love. No point beating around the bush. I'll be tidier."

"Good."

"And what will *you* do?"

I pursed my lips.

"Yes, Gavin?"

Forcing myself, I mumbled: "Try to stop losing my temper with things."

"Halleluiah!"

She was impressed by my portraits. I got her liveliness into them. If I painted from photographs instead of sketches, I'd ask her to wear the clothes and assume the pose. More often than not she did this hilariously, which had its own added effect. The portraits won admiration at what everyone called Natasha's Gallery, where some sold for decent prices.

I was still earning a pittance, though, and poverty would get me feeling low. I brooded. In my mind shone a sunlit, pre-Thatcher economy with textile industries clothing us, farmers feeding us and miners digging coal to warm us and power Britain's busy industries. I needed someone to blame and didn't wonder if maybe it hadn't really been quite like that. I hated being dependent on Nia. Sometimes, I'd work myself up.

"What use are all these qualifications? Why did I work so hard for them? What has been the point?"

"Nothing is happening because there's a point, Gavin. It's just happening."

"There's more to life than just living, Nia."

"There is just living."

"That's not enough."

"'Course it is. You need exercise. Trust me, I'm a nurse. Go to the University Gym. It's free for you."

"Ach."

"You *will* get a proper job, you'll see, lovely boy. I'm sure of it." She'd put her arm round me. "It's just a question of time, love."

Sometimes it was hard to comfort me. If all else failed, she'd make me laugh by taking off modelling poses, assuming innocent, haughty or surprised postures, or alluring smiles. She did for glamour what Tommy Cooper did for magic.

She bought me humorous T-shirts, which I wore at home not to hurt her feelings. She bought a set of snapping, clockwork teeth and a clockwork nun whose tongue poked in and out.

★ ★ ★ ★ ★ ★ ★ ★ ★

She was right. I got a full-time job teaching in the F.E. College. Eventually, I got a promotion. In the meantime I got a house on rent and a cat and two Welsh-speaking kids, the second one coming hard on the heels of the first.

Nia got depressed.

Indonesia was massacring the East Timorese and things looked ugly in Kashmir but we had our own problems in 1999. Although money was coming in now, the recession over, Nia moped and cried and messed up her mascara – an excuse not to go out after all. She was like somebody else. She stared through the window of the house we took after marrying, gazing tearfully at rows of vegetables under trees laden with young, green apples. Around the paths were flowers we had chosen together from a book. On the lawn were balls, hoops and carts, a tiny tricycle, a plastic paddling pool. "You don't care, do you? You don't listen to a word? Bugger you, Gavin Griffiths, bugger you, bugger you. You don't care." Tears welled up.

"Of course I care, Nia. You trying to say I'm a monster?" I pulled a monster face. She didn't laugh. "Jesus, Nia, go out with your friends, will you? Force yourself. A few drinks and a laugh, a bit of dancing. It'll make all the difference. I'll hold the fort."

"You?" she sneered.

I had made it obvious that I didn't find stinking nappies and vomit very life improving. In fact, it didn't surprise me she'd got depressed. I helped where I could, shopping, washing, ironing. Now I took on more baby care, too, so she could go out. I was 'The New Man', and glad as hell there was no such thing as paternity leave yet. With some effort and a lot of nagging she finally made herself go out and meet her friends. Then she did so again. Soon she threw away the doctor's antidepressants.

"Nia, I don't mind staying in, but, to be honest, if you wouldn't mind not dancing so much with that tall bloke from the tax office – "

"Gavin, you can be sure, I'd never – "

"I am, but we're the only two that are sure, see. People talk."

"Oh. OK. Put your mind at rest."

The kids grew, settled in at school and enjoyed sports.

Nia became a ward sister. I got that promotion.

I helped in a campaign against six thousand proposed new homes for which there was no local demand. The demand came from an alarmingly sincere prime minister who centralised power and behaved as if he reigned by divine right, taking us into wars with the foreign policy of a disinfectant ad and voicing a bizarre, messianic commitment to save Africa. Yes, you've guessed it. I got political.

Nia accepted the government's attempt to quantify the quality of NHS care with an equanimity I couldn't muster in Education.

"They're trying to make quality into a product," I fumed, "calling us 'providers', business people telling us what to provide. Talk about standards and you're called right wing, an 'elitist'. Speak your mind and get your career threatened. It's obedience through political correctness and public sector jargon. How long will it be before we fear to speak our *political* minds? How can you be so apathetic?"

"Give it a rest, will you? You're like a bloody record."

"Do you wonder how things may be for our children?"

"Why not teach them to be happy, Gavin? Today is what counts."

"Even if you're waiting for a kidney transplant, Nia?"

"You're always doing this. It's infuriating. I'm not waiting for one, am I?"

"So your generalisations don't apply to everyone's life, then?"

"You're so bloody clever."

"When you ignore the signs your destination may not be the happy one you expect."

"Living for the future doesn't make anyone happy either."

"So why did you want me to buy life insurance?"

"If you don't mind, you probably haven't noticed, but I'm in the middle of cleaning the windows."

* * * * * * * * * *

We were accepted easily here when we bought the house, the neighbours pleased to welcome Welsh-speakers, though by now the language of the school is only Welsh because of county policy and God knows how long that will last. The majority here these days are English, fled from whatever invasions they escaped. 'Que sera, sera' is Nia's attitude.

"Nothing we can do about it, Gavin," she says.

"Book of Destiny fully written up, is it, Nia? I thought you believed things just happened."

"They do. But don't you sometimes feel things are *meant*, as well? You getting that clerical job, for instance. Without it we wouldn't have got that flat, and then we wouldn't have rented that house. Or maybe even got married. And they were looking for someone settled when you got this job. I mean, it's like all of a piece."

"You're saying that marrying me was inevitable. You didn't make a choice."

"I *chose*, yes, but it *feels* as if it was meant. And if it happened, then it was always going to happen, wasn't it? That's logic."

"You're saying that you choose to marry of your own free will but nothing you do in the marriage can be your fault because it was all always going to happen anyway?"

"But if it *did* happen, surely it was always *going to*? How can you get out of that?"

"Nia, we aren't *in* that. Words can insist that other words following them have to be true, but logic doesn't bring about marriages, or there probably wouldn't be any."

"Explain better."

"Logic can't *cause* anything, Nia. It is not involved in events. Events can be made the subject of logic *after* they have happened but logic isn't involved in making them happen. Things aren't predestined. Not even you and me being married."

She said: "You really *are* quite clever, Mr Griffiths."

My chest swelled. I forgave her political apathy.

"You sorry you ended up with me, then?" she asked.

"Is the Pope sorry he ended up with God?"

"Gerraway, I'm not *that* bad. Oi, what exactly do you mean?"

"Put your mind at rest. I talked to God. He wants us to be together."

"Well, that's all right then."

She looked puzzled. "But why do we *feel* as if things were meant, Gavin? You didn't explain that, why it *feels* that way. It does, doesn't it?"

I shrugged. "It does, I know. Maybe it's just the sense of the present becoming the past, life moving on. But *while* something is happening you can put your oar in. For example, unwanted developments for the sake of unwanted immigration – "

"Oh, put a sock in it. Everybody is labouring in the same field even if they have just arrived from somewhere else. Anyway, newcomers buy most of your pictures."

It was true, and not just the landscapes, either. Portraits of Nia hang all over the place. She is a known 'character', and yet she has such a reputation for common sense that it sometimes brings people to our house looking for her advice.

"Why do so many people want to get divorced, then, Mam?" asked our daughter.

"Because they don't take time to appreciate what they've got. They think life should be like a story in a bloody magazine."

"Do you have to swear, Mam?"

"Sorry."

"You know how you're always telling Dad he's old before his time? Does that mean you'll divorce him?"

"No, cariad. I'm afraid we're stuck with him."

Across the road is a water wheel that doesn't turn and a hump-backed bridge too small for the traffic it carries. These are visible between two grand trees that shelter our house from the road. In autumn their golden leaves are burnished by the setting sun heading for the sea a couple of miles away and sometimes I rush for my easel and paint as fast as I can, chasing the light. I paint the great wheel in last, lighter than it really is so as to be in keeping with what was there when I started, with what is already passed, and there emerges the flux that viewers recognise as sunset. These pictures don't entirely look like what they are, or aren't quite what they look like. They are sunsets that aren't threatened by time.

I don't contribute my views to journals anymore. They are yesterday's. What has happened here is already on its journey towards history. Attached by memory to a past I can't hold on to, I quote 'Cofio', by Waldo Williams, his famous lyric about 'the forgotten things of man's family', lost in time, where 'the ordinary words of vanished languages, sweet to the ear once, are summoned by no tongue now'.

"It's happening," I say.

Nia won't brook this. It makes her angry.

"There are more Welsh-speakers than ever in Cardiff and Swansea. It's *change*, Gavin. Everything changes. Even you. Your Welsh has changed, and your accent. What happened to the working class hero I married? You've got a beard. Did I marry a bloody beard?"

"Working class? Do you mean those productive people that had real jobs and used to keep their families without handouts? They've vanished, Nia, gone, gone, along with a couple of hundred years of radical culture. Our roots!"

"But we've got Polish delicatessens now, though, instead of roots, see. Haven't we? Oh, Gavin *bach*, my poor boy, where can a little Welshman escape to? New Zealand is full of Chinese, they say – that's where the Welsh are emigrating, by the way, there and Australia."

"Well, fuck it. Let's join them. Make a new start. It's all too depressing here. Not even Plaid Cymru gives a damn anymore. It's just like all the other parties now. Let's go to Australia, it's cold in New Zealand."

"Tomorrow. Let's go to town tonight. I wanna dance."

"Aw, no, Nia."

"Yes, you grumpy old bugger."

"Don't you like my beard, then?"

"Your beard is fine. Just stop grumping all the time."

"Hell, Nia, you got to understand how it is, girl," I start, jokingly affecting the broad accent I had when we met and shaking my head, "what with the old Council Tax doubled now and the pensions all gone bust – "

"And immigration, don't forget that."

"I'll try not to, Nia."

"No vote allowed on the EU. Brussels wanting a bloody anthem."

"Country's going to the dogs."

"You could die of MRSA picking me up from work."

"I may want to."

"It's Saturday tomorrow. We can all go to the White Lion for lunch and watch Wales play France."

* * * * * * * * * *

Saturday is a fantastic day. Wales wins the Grand Slam for the second time in three years.

Nia reigns like a queen in the pub, soberer than when she was young but still loud and entertaining, mimicking the world, making it even more absurd yet somehow better. She still enjoys the good fortune of her looks – no chicken fillets in that bra. With her dress-sense modified at the insistence of a ten-year old daughter she looks better than ever.

She looks a million dollars.

However, you've realised by this time that it's not just that. And while her humour makes us a happy family, it's not that, either.

It's the way she drags her husband on to the dance floor laughing at the embarrassment of our kids.

We might be dead tomorrow. Today Nia dances.

I look up from my newspaper. "Identity cards next, Nia. Soon there'll be computer links between every authority with a file on us. It's coming."

"If you're gonna start a revolution we need more life insurance."

She hasn't changed one bit. I hope she never will. Her faults are as incurable as the London Orbital, but they don't matter, not when she can banish woes with a wink.

Her life is a celebration. That's what keeps our lives going. That's what I love. In a word, *her*.

Is that a consolation, or what?

What kind of a story are we meant to be living, anyway?

"A wise and tender portrait of ordinary
lives slipping slowly out of kilter with
the brave new world around them."
John Williams
Author of *Cardiff Dead* and *Michael X*

Bumping
Tony Bianchi

"Reveals an amazing eye for detail. His portrayals of old Tom and of
teenagers Barry and Nicky… are classics." **Morning Star**

www.alcemi.eu

TALYBONT CEREDIGION CYMRU SY24 5HE
e-mail gwen@ylolfa.com
phone (01970) 832 304
fax 832 782

ALCEMI Λ